OFF THE BEADIN' PATH

A Glass Bead Mystery

JANICE PEACOCK

Vetrai Press

Lafayette, California

2017

For Jeff

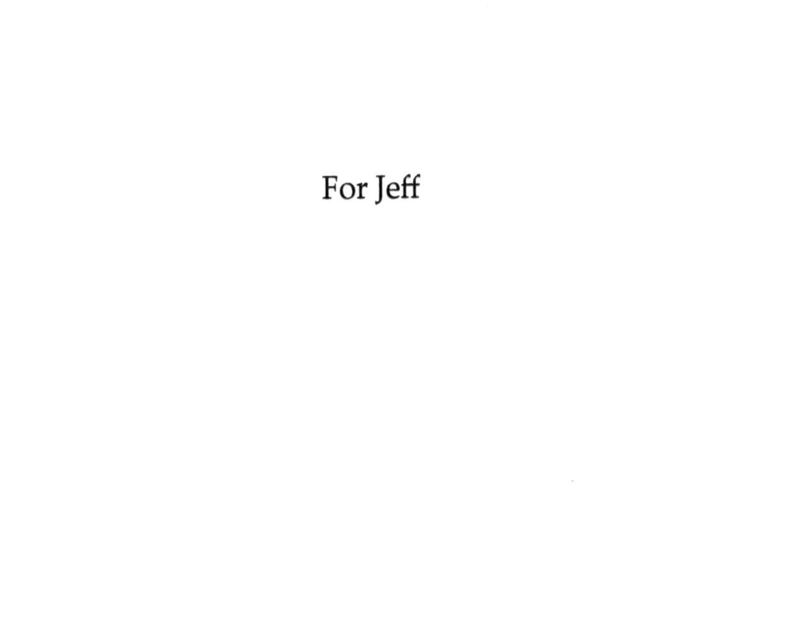

BOOKS BY JANICE PEACOCK

High Strung, Glass Bead Mystery Series, Book One

A Bead in the Hand, Glass Bead Mystery Series, Book Two

Off the Beadin' Path, Glass Bead Mystery Series, Book Three

To Bead or Not to Bead, Glass Bead Mystery Series, Book Four

Be Still My Beading Heart, A Glass Bead Mini-Mystery

ONE

THE RED AND BLUE LIGHTS of a police car behind us flashed through the van's windows as we hit Seattle's city limits. Tessa rolled down her window, while the police officer who pulled us over walked along the driver's side of her minivan, his boots crunching in the gravel as he approached.

"License and registration," the officer said, even before he bent to look in the window. His deep voice sent a familiar tingle down my spine.

I rummaged through the messy glove compartment, looking for the van's registration slip while Tessa rifled through her wallet for her driver's license. Finding the slip, I silently passed it to her. Tessa glanced up at the officer as she handed him the items he'd requested.

"Tessa, is that you? Jax?" Ryan Shaw asked, leaning down and peering into the van. He was one of Seattle's newest police officers and had apparently been assigned to the least satisfying job—parking and traffic. When Tessa and I met him in Portland, Oregon, a few months ago at a bead bazaar, he was a lowly security guard hoping to become a cop. While Tessa spent only a short while with Ryan during our time in Portland, I had gotten to know him quite well, but not as well as either of us would have liked. I'd been looking forward to seeing him once he moved to Seattle. But in the couple of phone calls we'd had since he'd relocated, both of which I'd initiated, he explained how busy he was getting settled and starting his new challenging position. I wondered if his feelings for me had cooled, and I was becoming unsure of how I felt about Ryan.

"Ryan! What are you doing here?" I asked. "I mean—you pulled us over, so I know what you're doing here, but—"

"Tessa was going forty-five in a twenty-five-mile-per-hour zone," Ryan said. Tessa was a notoriously fast driver, so this news was not surprising.

"Fortunately, you're such a terrific guy, and you know us, so you're going to let us off with a warning, right?" I asked.

"I'm serious about enforcing the law. If you commit a crime on my watch, you're going to have to deal with the consequences. Now, Tessa, I'm sorry, but I'm going to need to give you a ticket. It's nothing personal." Tessa covered her face with her hands and took a deep rattling breath. I looked up at Ryan, pleading silently.

"*Che casino*," Tessa said with a quiet whimper, switching to her native language, as she often did in times of stress, or when she was drunk. *Che casino* meant "what a mess" in Italian, and she was right, it was a mess. Tessa and I got into plenty of messes, especially since I'd moved to Seattle three years ago.

"Look what you've done to my friend!" I said, putting a comforting hand on Tessa's shoulder.

"I'm sorry." Ryan handed Tessa her license and registration. Maybe she wasn't going to get a ticket after all. Thank goodness! Of course Ryan wouldn't ticket my best friend. "You'll be getting the ticket in the mail," Ryan said as gently as possible. He came around to my side of the van. I rolled down my window, although I was in no mood to talk with him right now.

"How are you? Can we get together sometime?" he asked, leaning down so that his face was inches from mine. His olive skin and close-cropped dark hair were as perfect as ever.

"Uh, well, Ryan, I…" I looked up into those beautiful, chocolate brown eyes and nearly melted. Could I really say no to those sexy eyes, and the sexy everything else that made Ryan Shaw such a perfect specimen of manhood? "You know what? No! We can't get together. You gave Tessa a ticket. You haven't been in touch for months. Sorry," I said, pushing the button to roll up the window. Ryan unhooked his fingers from the edge of the glass as the window slid shut. I gave him a little wave. "Punch it, Tessa."

"I'm not going to punch it, but I will get the hell out of here. I don't want to get two speeding tickets in the space of fifty yards."

I looked in the van's side mirror as Tessa drove away. Ryan was standing at the side of the road, scratching his head. I don't think anyone—any woman, at least—had ever said no to that man. I was the first, and I was proud of myself. But, damn, he sure did have broad shoulders.

TWO

TESSA PULLED HER VAN into the space behind my house, right next to the Ladybug, my lovely red VW convertible. As we entered the studio through the back door, we were confronted with the mess I'd created during these last few frenzied weeks while I was getting ready for upcoming craft fairs. After moving to Seattle, I'd taken up glass beadmaking as a profession. I'd plunged into it wholeheartedly, selling my beads and jewelry at art festivals and in local boutiques. At first, I'd struggled to differentiate myself from the cheap, mass-produced imports, but as I got better and people started to understand the time and skill that went into making hand-crafted glass beads, my sales picked up. I was skilled enough, and well-known enough, that I was starting to make a small, but steady, income from my beads and jewelry.

My cat, Gumdrop, had settled into the toastiest spot in the whole house. Today he was sprawled in front of the large windows in my studio trying to absorb any sunlight that peeked through the clouds. That location had an advantage. If the clouds obscured all the sunshine, he could hop down onto the heating vent with minimal effort, blocking all the heat to my studio while keeping his belly nice and warm. He rolled over and stretched his paws out in front of him, spilling the contents of a few shallow white dishes I'd set up with the components to make a necklace for a custom order.

"We'll only be gone during the day, so be a good boy," I told my cat, giving him a little tummy rub. "We promise we'll come back every night to feed you." He started purring and melted into a puddle of gray fluff among the piles of beads on the table.

Tessa dropped her small red suitcase in my spare bedroom, which was also my overflow bead storage area. Tessa liked to call this room the "Bead Lair." She was fortunate to have her suitcase after it had been nearly hauled away by an overly-enthusiastic camp counselor a few hours earlier.

•   •   •

I'd started the day at the artful home Tessa shared with her husband, Craig, and their three children. They lived in the quiet Seattle neighborhood of Ballard, not too far from Tessa's beadmaking studio in the Fremont District.

"I think sending Izzy and Ashley to camp for spring break will be a positive experience," I said, tossing Tessa's suitcase into the minivan's trunk. "That way they won't get into trouble, like you know they would if they stayed home while we're off taking a class out in the middle of nowhere."

"I'm worried the girls are going to be miserable. A whole week at theater camp...how do I know they'll like it?"

"They both certainly have a flair for the dramatic, so they should do quite well," I said, doing my best to hide the sarcasm in my voice.

"At least I know Joey will be fine, since Benny will be with him at Camp Grammy," Tessa said. Benny was the son of a young couple we knew who had recently gotten back together after a few years apart. The boys had become fast friends last year during the grand opening festivities at a local bead store, and after that weekend, they were nearly inseparable. As we entered the house, Joey and Benny ran toward us.

"Are you big guys ready to go?" Tessa asked, kneeling to greet them.

"Yeah! Let's go!" the boys shouted, slamming into Tessa's open arms, nearly knocking her over. At five years old, they bubbled with enthusiasm about nearly everything except eating green beans. I hoped they didn't lose their energetic spirit anytime soon and that they'd eventually become more enthusiastic about veggies.

"I'll go get the girls," I said, heading up the staircase toward their room. The door to the teens' room was shut. I knocked. "Izzy? Ashley?"

No answer. I tried again. "Izzy? Ashley? Can I come in?"

"I don't want to go," Izzy said with a groan.

"Ditto," Ashley said, sounding equally pained.

"I'm coming in!" I pushed the door open. The girls were sprawled on their beds. Each of them looked like they were in agony, arms thrown across their beds in despair. "Come on, girls. It's not going to be that bad. You might like theater camp."

"I don't understand why we can't stay here. We're old enough to be by ourselves," said Izzy, who, at seventeen, probably was old enough to stay at home by herself. But, when combined with sixteen-year-old Ashley, Tessa's daughters were far too volatile to leave alone if we expected the house to be standing when we returned.

"No, sorry. What your mom says, goes," I said, picking up their duffel bags and leaving their room. "Time to go."

Dragging their heels, they followed me.

"I'm not your Sherpa. You can carry your own bags," I told the girls, dropping the bags at their feet at the top of the staircase. The girls took the bags and dragged them down the stairs, heaved them into the back of the van, then continued their protest by sitting on the back bumper and looking at me darkly.

"I'm not the one making you go to camp," I said, which was, in fact, untrue. I had insisted Tessa's kids go to camp to ensure this week would be as hassle-free as possible. During our disastrous trip to Portland, Tessa's daughters had fought like wild animals at home, causing her so much anguish that she couldn't enjoy her time at the Bead Fun sale. That, and the fact that I'd found a dead body, had made it a particularly stressful weekend. With her kids at camp and her husband on a fishing trip, I hoped Tessa would have a distraction-free week taking a glassblowing class with me.

Tessa locked up the house and came down to join us. Joey and Benny were already in the van and had buckled themselves into their booster seats.

"Let's go! Let's go!" both boys chanted while clapping their hands.

"They have the right idea. Let's go!" Tessa said as she swung herself behind the wheel.

With an audible sigh, Tessa's daughters climbed into the very back of the van, and I jumped in the front seat next to Tessa. The little boys chattered away while the girls were silent, each staring out their own window, sulking.

We headed first for Camp Grammy, also known as Craig's mother's house. She lived on the Olympic peninsula, an hour's drive from Seattle. We took the ferry across to Bremerton and out to Sequim, which all the newcomers and tourists called *SEEquim*, but locals called *Squim*. I'd been calling it *Squim* for at least a year, which meant that I'd finally lived in the Pacific Northwest long enough to feel, and talk, like a local. When I'd first moved here from Miami, I felt like a fish out of water—a tropical fish, to be precise. These days, I've adapted to life here in Seattle, Washington, with its cold, wet weather, but I still relish a sunny afternoon, knowing that it will soon be gone and replaced by rain clouds.

Heading off the main road, we finally turned toward what we had been calling Camp Grammy for weeks leading up to this. Craig's mom, Patsy, greeted us on the front porch as Tessa pulled up to the rustic house.

"Grammy!" Joey called, unlatching the seatbelt on his booster seat.

"Just a minute, Joey," said Tessa. "Wait until I can open the door." As soon as it was open, Joey launched himself out of the van, with Benny following close behind.

"Are you girls getting out?" Tessa asked Izzy and Ashley.

"Yeah, I guess so," Izzy said, crawling out of the van.

Patsy came around the side of the van to greet the girls.

"Oh, my beautiful granddaughters! I wish you were spending the week with me! We could have so much fun cooking and sewing," Patsy said, pulling the girls into a hug.

"Sorry, Grammy," Izzy said.

"Yeah, sorry," Ashley said.

They weren't sorry. I was certain that the girls thought the only thing worse than a week singing and dancing at theater camp would be a week cooking and sewing with their grandmother.

"Mom!" Tessa gave her mother-in-law a kiss on the cheek. Patsy awkwardly tried to kiss her back. "I'm sorry I can't stay, I've got to get the girls to their camp by eleven," Tessa said, planting a second kiss on her mother-in-law's cheek, which Patsy wasn't quite ready for, belatedly kissing the air after Tessa had already moved on. Even after all the years Tessa had been married to her son, Pasty still wasn't sure if it was one kiss or two when she greeted her Italian daughter-in-law.

"I'm looking forward to spending time with the boys. Maybe I can plan something for another time with Izzy and Ashley. What's Craig doing while you take your class?"

"He's going fishing out in Puget Sound," Tessa said. Her husband had decided to take the week off, as well, while contractors worked on their house.

"You'd better get going. I'll keep these boys occupied out here in the woods," Patsy said.

Tessa approached Joey, who was sitting on the stump of a log, watching ants with Benny. She gave him a big hug. "You be a good boy and listen to Grammy Patsy. You, too, Benny," she said, ruffling his hair. The boys were so focused on the ants that it seemed like the best plan would be to get out of there while they were distracted, so there would be no teary-eyed goodbyes.

We got on the road and headed toward Camp White Horse. Tessa had chosen this camp for the girls while we took a class at a glass-blowing studio east of Seattle. Initially, Tessa told her daughters they would be staying at Patsy's. The girls didn't seem to mind until Patsy got on the phone and told them her plans to teach them to sew and make beef stew.

"Please, Mom," the girls had pleaded, "find us something else to do. Anything. We'll do it and we won't complain." Tessa chose theater camp for them, and so far, the girls hadn't complained much, but their level of sullenness was rising to epic proportions as we headed into the final leg of our journey.

Tessa turned down a long narrow side road, following the glitter-covered arrow on a signpost. After a few bumpy miles on a gravel road, the main gates of the camp appeared. Decorated with silver balloons and gigantic comedy and tragedy masks, the entrance looked a little less like the horse ranch that it normally was.

Tessa rolled down her window as a counselor dressed in a tuxedo approached the van.

"Hi, and welcome to Camp White Horse! Or, as we're calling it this week, Camp Broadway!" She started clapping and hopping up and down, which was a little too much enthusiasm for me. "We would like to take the campers right away and get started with some trust exercises."

Another tuxedo-clad woman opened the van's sliding door, took the reluctant girls by the hand, and pulled them out. A young man wearing a black silk top hat with a rhinestone-studded brim grabbed the luggage out of the back of the van and slammed the doors.

"Okay, thanks so much for dropping off your girls. We'll take good care of them!" said the first counselor, giving us a sweeping bow.

I noticed that the counselor with the top hat was carrying an extra bag—one that didn't belong to the girls.

"Tessa? Is that your suitcase?"

"Oh no! Wait!" Tessa shouted, jumping out of the van and running to rescue her small red suitcase from the man. She gave each girl a last hug, reluctantly turned back to the van, threw the suitcase in the back seat, and climbed in the driver's seat. "I'm lucky you noticed they were taking my bag. I wouldn't want to be without it this week."

Ashley and Izzy looked over their shoulders at their mother and me, their eyes wide and their lips tight, as they were swept away by a gang of sparkly penguins.

• • •

"*Yoo-hoo, yoo-hoo!*" Val called out as she let herself in the front door and sashayed down the hall to my studio. "Tessa, you get to be roomies with me and Jax this week, how fun is that?"

Stanley the basset hound bounded in behind Val, nearly knocking her off her four-inch red patent leather stilettos when he didn't stop in time. Strictly speaking, Val was not my roommate. Only Gumdrop held that title. She was my neighbor—actually, my tenant—who lived mere inches from me in our Craftsman-style duplex.

"Hi, you sweet boy," Tessa said, giving Stanley a vigorous scratch on the head. He flopped onto the floor, looking like a misshapen bearskin—basset skin—rug. I was certain there would be a puddle of drool left on my oak flooring when he got up.

"Where's Gumdrop?" Val asked. We were always careful about keeping Gumdrop and Stanley separate, since there were still moments when the cat insisted this house was not just his home but his country, and the dog was an invader who must be stopped at all costs.

"He's down at the end of my worktable, sunning himself by the window," I said.

"Oh good, because I really, really, really don't want to deal with all the howling and fighting," Val said.

"Sounds like my house," Tessa said. "But not this week. Everyone is off having fun away from everyone else. We've got some contractors coming in to do some remodeling work. They're opening the attic to make a new room for Izzy. She and Ashley have been fighting so much lately that I've decided that we'll all have more peace and quiet if those two aren't sharing the same bedroom."

"Have you ever thought about turning your attic into an extra room?" Val asked me, looking toward the door at the top of the stairs, against the wall that separates my studio from the rest of the house.

"It's only Gumdrop and me. I don't need the space."

"But think about it, if you had a room up in the attic, visitors could stay in it, and you wouldn't have to give up the Bead Lair," Tessa said.

I had thought about it from time to time, but had always dismissed the concept. The idea of spending any amount of time in the spider-infested attic gave me the heebie-jeebies. I'd only entered it once to grab some tiles that must've been stored there for decades. Other than the overall spookiness of the attic, the other thing holding me back was a lack of funds for the renovation.

The advantage of finishing off the space would be that I'd have an additional storage area, since I didn't have a garage. That wasn't a big deal when I first moved here because I only brought what I could fit in my car, including Gumdrop. Now that I'd been living here for a few years, things were starting to accumulate, and my living space was getting tighter and tighter.

"I think some night this week we're going to have to take a look in your attic," Tessa said, picking up some of the beads that Gumdrop had knocked onto the floor.

"It's scary up there! It's full of boxes covered in dust and cobwebs and pieces of furniture covered in sheets. They look like ghosts," I said.

"You have ghosts?" Val asked.

"No, I don't have ghosts, they only look like ghosts."

"Oh, good, because I was about to go and get my perfume," Val said.

We learned about Val's cure for the common ghost last fall when we were staying at the supposedly-haunted Red Rose Hotel. She liberally spritzed the hotel room with her somewhat questionable Chanel No. 6, which, according to Val and the guy on the street corner who sold it to her, was better than No. 5.

Tessa blew her bangs out of her eyes, a sure sign of exasperation. With Val around, you had to get used to her funny notions about how the world worked. If Val believed in something, no matter how unlikely, there was no way you could get her to change her mind. It was one of the most adorable things about Val, and one of the most aggravating.

"So, ladies, are you hungry for some dinner?" Val asked. "I made some super-yummy chili, and it's ready to eat right next door."

"Sorry, I think we better head over to the glassblowing studio," Tessa said.

"Oh, too bad. You'd love it. You want to know my secret ingredient?" Val asked, turning to leave. "Chocolate!" Stanley jumped up and followed her, stumbling over his ears as he went. Sure enough, he left a puddle of drool behind.

"I'd love to get the recipe from you. My kids will eat anything with chocolate and so will I," Tessa called after her.

"I'll email the recipe to you. Bye, darlings. Have fun at your class," Val said, shutting the door behind her.

"Here, let me show you something that will get you excited about the class," Tessa said. She pulled out an elegant marbled-paper box from her purse. Gently untying its satin ribbon, she opened the package, and I looked inside, feeling like I was peeking into a special box of chocolates. Inside was a stunning strand of Venetian beads.

"Oh, Tessa, these beads are gorgeous!" I plucked the exquisite necklace from the box. Each bead was covered in a mosaic pattern of multicolored flower designs. The satin surface of the beads hinted at their age. They were certainly not new.

"It was my nonna's. The design is called *millefiori*. It means 'a thousand flowers' in Italian," Tessa said, taking the necklace from me and holding it near the studio window. We admired the beads in the sunlight, even though there wasn't much of it. The skies had been threatening rain all day.

"I love the tiny details in the flowers. I can't believe we're actually going to learn to make this kind of bead in the workshop," I said.

"It should be a lot of fun. I'm excited about it."

"I'm a little nervous. I've never been in a glassblowing studio before. At least you spent time hanging around glassblowers when you moved to Venice after high school, plus all those summers you visited your grandparents in Murano."

"You'll be fine. There's nothing to worry about. I promise," Tessa said.

As it turned out, Tessa was wrong. There would be plenty to worry about.

THREE

THE GLASSBLOWING STUDIO was in the town of Carthage, a forty-five-minute drive from Seattle. Tessa and I decided to drive the Ladybug each day rather than stay locally, since the distance didn't seem too daunting and the drive would give us time to gossip before and after class. We'd heard some of the students decided to camp near the glassblowing shop to save money. That wasn't an option for Tessa and me. We were too old for that. In fact, I think I've always been too old for camping.

The owners, Dez and Abby McCabe, named their workshop Old Firehouse Studio, which made sense because it was, in fact, the old firehouse in Carthage. They had spent the last two years building out the space and installing glassblowing equipment and were now making their own glass art vases and paperweights. Recently they had begun offering glassblowing classes. Since Seattle real estate was expensive, having a business in the boondocks made sense. Properties in this area were less expensive, but it also seemed like it would be difficult to attract visitors, especially since there wasn't much out here except for Old Firehouse Studio. Correction: There was nothing else out here.

"What? No Starbucks?" Tessa asked as I turned off the highway into Carthage. How would she survive a week without a constant supply of coffee?

"Not every town in America has a Starbucks," I said. Of course, all I could think was that Seattle could do with fewer coffee shops and that it would be convenient if one simply relocated here, immediately. "Don't panic. We'll make coffee at my house in the morning. We can leave a little early each day and get a cup on the road, too."

"But what about our ten o'clock cup?" asked Tessa. "Our two o'clock cup? What about that cup at four o'clock when it's been a really long day?"

"Maybe the studio will have a coffee maker. We aren't the only ones around here who love a good cup of java," I said.

Old Firehouse Studio wasn't hard to find. It was at the end of the main street, called, appropriately enough, Main Street. I pulled into a parking spot by a garage-sized door at the front of the building. The door was rolled open and through it was the glassblowing studio, known by those in the glass world as the hot shop. Tessa and I got out of the car and stood at the entrance, taking it all in. We stepped tentatively inside. The workshop was set up differently from what we used when we made glass beads—bigger, hotter, and, I must admit, scarier. Instead of a pistol-sized torch attached to a table and a kiln not much bigger than a toolbox, the hot shop was filled with huge furnaces of molten glass and kilns the size of refrigerators. At one end of the room was a glassblower's bench, a seat with two parallel metal rails on each side. The devices on the shelf attached to the bench looked more like torture implements than tools for forming glass.

Blown glass hummingbird feeders strung from fishing line hung in the floor-to-ceiling windows next to the rolling door. Had there been sun on this April day, I'm sure the colorful globes would have glistened. Instead, they glowed dimly, illuminated by the gray sky of a Washington spring.

A woman exited the office at the back of the studio and extended her hand.

"Abby McCabe," she said with a firm shake, "Here for the class?" The woman was about my age, but thin and wiry, and strong—stronger than I'd ever be. She was wearing a sleeveless T-shirt that revealed her ropey biceps.

"Yes, I'm Jax O'Connell, and this is Tessa Ricci," I said.

"Welcome to Old Firehouse Studio. I'm so glad you're able to join us for this class. You two haven't worked in the hot shop before, have you? Don't worry, we'll give you a little orientation. Let me get Sam, he's our gaffer," Abby said. Noticing my confusion, she added, "A gaffer is the head glassblower in a studio. In our studio, he's the only glassblower, other than Dez. Sam will show you around."

"Sam!" Abby screeched. "I gotta yell at him," she explained, "otherwise he doesn't hear me when he's working out back."

Sam entered the studio through the back door next to the office, coming in from what looked like a utility yard. Sam was stocky with a scruffy beard and looked to be in his early thirties.

"Sam, this is Jax and Tessa. They're new to the hot shop. Why don't you get them oriented?"

"Hey, nice to meet you. I'm Sam Tilden. I'm the lead glassblower here, and I'm happy to help you any way I can. First off, we've got some rules here in the hot shop. You're going to have to wear cotton clothing."

"We're glass beadmakers, so we know fire and synthetic fabrics don't mix," Tessa said. I was glad Tessa was doing what she could to assure Sam we weren't complete newbies when it came to hot glass.

"Okay. Good to know. Still, you'll probably want to wear long sleeves to protect your arms from the heat." I noticed he was wearing a short-sleeved shirt, which was covered in dark burn marks. Some were big enough to have become holes, others were still small black dots. "You won't see any of us wearing long sleeves, but we've been at this a long time and can handle the heat. These furnaces are hot. You don't have to touch anything to get burned. Standing near the furnace for too long can do it. While you're learning, we don't want you rushing, and we don't want you to get injured."

I'd been burned plenty of times, but only on my fingers, and most of those burns were no worse than I'd get by touching the edge of a hot pan in the oven. I'd been hit by a few rice-sized pieces of glass that had popped off glass rods I was melting with my torch. But compared to what could happen in a hot shop, the dangers in a glass beadmaking studio were minimal. When making glass beads, it didn't matter whether you wore long sleeves or not; you could wear anything you wanted, as long as you chose natural fibers that wouldn't melt if you got too close to a heat source.

"You'll want to wear closed-toed shoes. Trust me when I say that you don't want molten glass falling on your feet," Sam said, pointing at his own scuffed-up work boots.

Tessa and I nodded in agreement. Molten glass on any part of the body was a very bad thing.

"This is the furnace." We walked over to an upright concrete cylinder, which was a little smaller than the Ladybug. "Inside it's 2,100 degrees, and we keep it like that twenty-four hours a day, seven days a week." An eighteen-inch square door was located at chest height on the front of the furnace. The gaps between the door and its frame glowed bright orange. Behind the small door was a crucible of molten glass. Its extreme heat, combined with the vibrant yellow heating elements, lit up the inside of the furnace.

A vintage white Chevy pickup pulled into the parking lot out front. A small, fit man slid out of the cab and headed into the hot shop. I recognized him from the studio's website. This was Dez McCabe, and he owned the studio with his wife, Abby.

"Dez," he said, extending his hand to Tessa and then to me.

"Hi, I'm Jax, and this is Tessa," I said.

"Nice to meet you both. Hope this class isn't going to be too hard for you, since you're middle…"

"Uh, Dez? Can I speak with you privately," Abby broke in, and then to Sam, "Can you keep showing these gals the studio?"

Dez ambled toward the office with Abby.

"Was Dez about to call us middle-aged?" I asked Tessa, offended. Even though I was approaching middle-age, I didn't think it needed to be pointed out publicly.

"Look, Jax, you've got to understand, glassblowing is hard, physically. Most people who are first-timers are a lot younger than we are," said Tessa. She and I both had reached our mid-forties in decent shape, other than my serious case of studio-butt from sitting in front of my torch, instead of power-walking with Val when she took her dog for a spin around the neighborhood.

"It's not like we've got one foot in the grave or anything!"

"I know, and we do have experience working in glass, only on a much smaller scale."

"On a way, way smaller scale." I was already nervous about taking this class, and now I felt like I had been told I was too old to do it. It didn't make me happy.

"I'm not ready to give up before we've even started. Are you?"

I knew Tessa was right. I needed to step outside my comfort zone. The best things in my life have happened because I've stepped away from a place where I felt safe and in control. It was that way when I moved here. I knew I needed to make a change from my less-than-amazing life in Miami if I didn't want to be stuck in an apartment with a leaky sink and harvest gold appliances forever. My boyfriend at the time, Jerry, had started spending more time in front of the TV and less time with me. I didn't want to be with a man who had been ignoring me for years, only saying, "Hi, babe," and, "Bye, babe," each day. If I waited too long to order take-out, he would add exponentially to the word count of the day by asking, "What's for dinner?"

But even more than leaving Jerry, I'd wanted to start a new life away from the cold, white walls of my job at Clorox. I wanted to create beautiful glass objects and become my authentic, creative self. Leaving Jerry and driving to Seattle was the biggest challenge I'd ever faced, and now here I was, looking at a smaller challenge, learning to blow glass, which was relatively easy compared to moving cross-country. I took courage in reminding myself how much I had accomplished. I had even started up my own company, Ladybug Beads, and was managing to keep myself afloat financially.

"You're right. I want to do this. I can do this," I told Tessa.

"Of course you can," she said, beaming at me.

"Are these blowpipes?" I asked Sam, pointing to a few four-foot-long, inch-thick metal pipes that were resting against the wall. Each pipe was tapered on one end and flared out on the opposite end.

"Yes, they are. The blowpipes are tubes; they're what we use to blow glass into hollow shapes like vases. We blow into the tapered end." He pointed to another set of metal rods nearby, which were more slender than the blowpipes. "These are punties. They don't have a hole that runs through them. They're used as handles when you're creating solid glass items like paperweights, or canes like we'll be making this week."

Sam passed a punty to each of us to examine. I was fascinated to see this equipment because it was quite different from what I'd seen in the glassblowing workshop at Clorox, where I'd first learned about working with hot glass. Scientific glassblowers usually work with rods or tubes of borosilicate glass that they heat in a torch and then form into apparatus for experiments and research. That setup differed from art glass studios like this one, where glassblowers pulled clear molten glass out of a furnace and shaped it into vases, paperweights, and many other decorative and functional objects.

"This is the marver," Sam continued, running one of his hands across the top of a metal platform the size and height of a picnic table. "We roll the hot glass on it to shape it." I used a hand-held graphite marver when I made glass beads. It seemed to me that glass beadmakers used a lot of the same tools as glassblowers, except that everything we used was on a much smaller scale.

"That certainly puts my little hand-held marver to shame. I guess when you're making big pieces, you need a big marver to shape them," I told Tessa.

The office door slammed open with a crash. Abby ran from the office, jumped in Dez's truck, and was gone.

Dez stomped out of the office.

"That damn woman! She makes me crazy!" Dez yelled, pounding a fist on the office's doorjamb.

"Excuse me, ladies. I think I need to see what I can do to help

Dez," Sam said. "We'll finish the tour a bit later." Sam joined Dez as he stormed around in the office screaming idle threats—at least I hoped they were idle—at Abby, who wasn't around to hear his tirade.

"What do you think that's about?" I asked as we headed outside to get away from Dez's ranting. Tessa and I took a seat on a low bench in front of the studio's roll-up door.

"I don't know, but I hope it doesn't mean we're in for a week of drama," Tessa said, zipping up her hooded sweater. As the day wore on it was getting colder, and the clouds were threatening rain. "I could use a lot less drama in my life. I was hoping this week away from Izzy and Ashley would be stress-free."

A muddy Greyhound bus squealed to a stop near the café a couple of blocks away. Two young women dragged their suitcases down its stairs and looked around. As the bus took off, it left them in a cloud of exhaust. They waved their thin, pale hands in front of their faces and started their slow march toward the studio. It was the Twins. They were not actual twins, but rather two women who had chosen to look nearly identical. I had never been able to tell them apart. They weren't wearing their usual long, flowing black skirts, instead sporting black skinny jeans, black T-shirts, and enough black eye-liner to make a raccoon jealous. They'd had this Goth look for as long as I'd known them, and their jewelry reflected their funereal fashion sense. Around each of their necks hung black glass pendants adorned with miniature dancing skeletons made of seed beads.

"Hi, Sara. Hi, Lara," Tessa and I said as the Twins approached the studio. "Good trip?"

"Revolting," one of them said. They dropped their bags on the studio floor and looked around, scowling.

"What a vile town, if you can call it that," said the other. "There's almost nothing here."

Sam left Dez in the office and introduced himself to the Twins.

"We're waiting for a couple more people, so let me show you the rest of the facility, and we'll come back and look at the hot shop a little more once everyone else gets here," Sam said.

"Over here is the break room. We've got some lockers in here, where you can leave your stuff. On the other side of the lockers is a bathroom with a shower, for those folks who are camping," Sam told us. "The campsite is out through the utility yard, which leads to the field in back."

We looked into the utility yard, an asphalt covered work area beneath a corrugated roof. At the far end of the yard was a set of two rolling doors, similar to what we'd seen in the hot shop, with a drive-up ramp that I assumed they used to facilitate unloading of heavy supplies and equipment into the storage area. Inside one of the open doors were industrial shelving units full of spare parts, sacks of raw glass, and tools. Off to the right, a field sloped down to the river. Two rusty trailers sat off to one side of the field. The downhill edge of each was propped up on cinder blocks to keep it level.

"Are any of you going to camp?" Sam asked.

"Oh, not us," said Tessa. "We're much too …" then realizing that she didn't want to point out how old we were said, "I mean, we could camp, but Jax has a cat we need to feed, and well, we need to be able to go home at night." This was a complete lie, since Val could easily come over and dump some cat food in Gumdrop's bowl any time, and often did when I wasn't home.

"We've got a cottage," Lara, or possibly Sara, said.

"Okay, you'll be in the one on the left, that's for our students. The one on the right, that's for the instructors." To me, cottage was a fancy name for what looked like a beat up old Airstream.

"We're going down to drop off our things," the other twin said.

They picked up their bags and headed down the muddy path toward their trailer, their army boots squelching as they tromped along.

Vance Dalton, who had given up calling himself Vandal last fall, arrived a little while later in his brown Corolla. He'd gotten a new pair of glasses, with Val's guidance, replacing the ones that were held together with duct tape. He'd slimmed down and was no longer sporting a tucked-in Hawaiian shirt. Instead, he had found himself a nice sage green Henley pullover, along with some new Levi's 501 jeans. Vance was looking good, and I could see he was feeling more confident, which was a change for the better.

"Jax! Tessa!" Vance said, enveloping us both in a bear hug.

"Careful," I said, pulling myself away from him before we got crushed.

"Hey, I'm Vance," he said to Sam. Sam greeted Vance with a fist bump. There was an immediate dude rapport between the two of them. "I brought my photography gear. Can I take some photos while we work this week?"

"Sure, bro," Sam said.

Another woman arrived around the same time Vance did.

"Everyone, this is Katia, she's one of my best students," Sam said. Katia was tall and thin, but lacked the hardness I'd seen in Abby. Even in jeans and a T-shirt, she had a refined and elegant style. Her long blonde hair was braided to keep it out of the way. It's not a good idea to have your hair loose when working with extreme heat. I'd learned that the hard way, after singeing my bangs off in a scorching hot kiln.

"Hey, hi, everyone. I'm delighted to be joining you. I love taking classes here. It's one of the best things that ever happened to me," Katia said.

And finally, Duke sauntered in. According to Tessa, he considered himself to be a big name in the glass world. After meeting him a few months ago, she'd told me he was a buffoon. Meeting him right now, I had to agree. Duke seemed to think he owned the place, or at least he felt entitled to act like it.

"Duke, Duke, Duke," he repeated to each of us as he shook our hands. If I'd been feeling more at ease, I would have started to sing the old 1960s song "Duke of Earl," but I thought better of it. Everyone already thought I was too old to be here, so breaking out a golden oldie would not be a good move. I was certain I'd be singing that silly song to myself for the rest of the night.

"So, now all we need is the instructor," said Dez, looking around, peeved, although it wasn't entirely clear if that was because the instructor was late or because Abby had bolted out the door and driven away in his car, most likely both.

A black Lincoln Town Car pulled up in front of the studio. Our instructor, Marco de Luca, had arrived. The driver popped the trunk and Marco grabbed his leather suitcase as well as an over-sized plastic toolbox. Dez and Abby had brought him in from Venice to teach this class. Tessa and I wondered why they would need to import someone from Italy when Seattle likely had as many excellent glassblowers as Venice. Abby told Tessa she was trying to build a reputation for bringing in high-quality instructors from around the world as a way to increase the profits for their new studio. It was a gamble on their part, but the payoff was potentially huge. If they could bring in paying students to learn from famous artists—who would be expensive to hire—their business could become profitable quickly. That is, if they could fill the classes. If they couldn't fill the classes with students willing to pay a premium to attend, Abby and Dez could lose a lot of money. I'll admit, while this class was more expensive than most, it seemed worth it. Otherwise, I would have had to fly to Venice to take a class with Marco de Luca, which would certainly not be affordable on my budget.

Marco strode into the glass studio. He was close to six feet tall and nicely built. If Val were here, she'd call him a hunk. He set down his bags on a metal table at the back of the room and took off his sunglasses to get a good look at his students. Wearing sunglasses on this dreary evening was obviously more of a fashion statement than a necessity.

"Where is Violetta?" Marco asked. His English was nearly perfect, except for a slight Italian accent. Abby and Dez had invited Violetta Canetti, a glass bead importer who specialized in selling Venetian glass beads, to come sell her wares during Marco's class and give a lecture on vintage Italian beads. She was touring the United States selling her beads and had been in New York prior to the class.

"She missed her flight," Dez said. "I got a text from her saying she'd get the next one. She should be here tomorrow."

"So typical of Violetta—always late. It is a good thing the important part of the class starts now that I am here," said Marco, pulling off his oversized charcoal-colored sweater. He was wearing a faded red T-shirt underneath, which was covered in brown burn marks like the ones we'd seen on Sam's tattered shirt, evidence of years of working with hot glass.

I turned to Tessa and whispered. "The important part. His part?"

"It's just how he is," Tessa replied, shrugging. "Typical Italian glassblower attitude."

Dez gathered everyone together.

"Welcome to our studio. Abby and I are delighted to have you here to take our first class with a guest instructor. And who better to start off our amazing class calendar than the internationally-renowned glass artist Marco de Luca? He'll lead a short introductory session tonight before we get started in earnest tomorrow with more lessons," Dez said. "Please make sure you come by my office and pay your balance on the class fees. I've got dinner taken care of tonight. You're on your own for the rest of your meals. We don't have much here in Carthage, but we do have the Robin's Nest Café down the street. We've also got Meat and Eat a few minutes' drive away. That's a sandwich shop. You might want to consider bringing your lunch, or you should feel free to cook here in the kitchen. We've got a hot plate and a microwave. We do have a coffee maker, but it's been on the fritz, so I'm not sure if it'll work or not."

Tessa and I looked at each other with wide eyes. We were reading each other's minds. How were we going to survive with no coffee?

FOUR

ABBY ARRIVED A FEW MINUTES LATER with two pizza boxes, an enormous bowl of Caesar salad, and a scowl on her face. It seemed that whatever she'd been fighting about with Dez was still troubling her. She headed for the break room and we followed.

"Anyone want wine? If you do, feel free to pick a hand-blown goblet from the shelf," Abby said. "Oh, and Marco, I hope the pizza feels like home for you, or at least that it isn't too terrible by your standards."

"Thanks for letting us use these glasses. They're absolutely stunning," I said, choosing a purple and green goblet from the collection of glasses on the shelf.

"You've got to use things that were made to be used," Tessa said, picking a fiery red glass.

"Did you make all of them?" I asked Abby.

"Me? No, Dez and Sam made most of these. I'm more the brains behind this outfit. I leave the artistic stuff up to those two."

"Now, Abby, you know you could make one of these," Dez said, choosing a stemmed glass with a wide yellow rim and filling it with wine. "You're a superb glassblower, just a little out of practice."

Marco opened one of the pizza boxes and looked tentatively inside.

"This is pizza, no?" he asked. He knew darn well it was pizza. "Looks like lasagna with very much cheese and not cooked enough." It seemed to me he was trying to be difficult.

"Sorry, we don't have an oven here so we can't do anything about that," said Abby, still angry with Dez, or someone else, I couldn't be sure.

"I will show you how the glassblowers cook in Venice. We have here, all the things. Is there a kiln that is hot?" Marco asked.

"Sure, number one on the left is up at 950 degrees," Sam said.

"That's a little hot," Marco said, grabbing a pizza box and some foil from the kitchen, then heading for the hot shop. He found a long-handled metal tray, covered it with foil and slid the pizza onto it. He opened the door to kiln number one and let out the heat within, turning his face away so he didn't get blasted. When the thermometer on the kiln dropped to 500 degrees, Marco slid the pizza into it. He shut the kiln door most of the way, the tray's handle protruding from the opening. We all watched as the temperature on the kiln increased slowly. If Marco didn't take the pizza out soon there'd be nothing left but charcoal.

"Do not worry. We'll get the pizza out in a moment," he said, responding to the concerned looks on our faces.

He opened the kiln door, grabbed the tray's handle, and carried the pizza triumphantly back to the break room. It looked absolutely delicious—crispy on the edges and covered in bubbling cheese. The Twins and Vance grabbed the other pizza and headed back into the hot shop to cook it as Marco had.

We all settled down to eat around the table in the kitchen while Abby filled our fancy stemware with red wine from a gallon jug. Marco took a swig of the wine and grimaced.

"Too bad you couldn't afford some decent wine," Marco said, looking disdainfully at Abby. She ignored him and kept pouring.

Tessa pulled out her phone. "Smile!" she said, pressing the camera button as I took a bite of pizza.

"That's going to be the worst picture ever!" I said, after swallowing.

I had a surprise for Tessa in the Ladybug. Her birthday was the previous Friday. Craig took her out to dinner, but I hadn't had a chance to see her during the craziness of preparing for this week. I'd decided to bring a cake to this gathering. While Tessa wasn't looking, I placed a three-layer chocolate cake in the trunk of my car. Val had baked it and I made her promise not to tinker with the recipe in any way—just chocolate, flour, and whatever else goes in a cake. I wasn't sure, because I was never much of a cook. Val fed me, and whatever she didn't make for me came from take-out or the local bakery. I'd always wondered why she never started a bakery of her own. If she would stop putting crazy ingredients in her concoctions, she'd be a superstar in the world of desserts. Heck, she already was to me.

I slipped outside and grabbed the tray that contained the cake, forks, plates, napkins, candles, and a knife. I wasn't sure what I'd find at the studio, so I'd come prepared. I knew we'd have a way to light the candles. Someone would have a lighter, matches, or even a torch.

I stepped into the kitchen with the cake. "Happy birthday, Tessa!"

"What a surprise, I can't believe you brought a cake all the way out here!" Tessa said.

"I couldn't let your birthday pass without a celebration," I said, leaning over and giving her a big smooch on the forehead.

"Let me light those candles for you," Sam said, pulling a lighter from his pocket.

We sang "Happy Birthday" to Tessa. I used my knife to cut slices of cake and then passed them around to everyone. Val had done it. She'd made the perfect chocolate cake with the thickest, richest frosting I'd ever tasted. I savored every bite. When I finished my piece of cake, I contemplated having another. But I knew if I did, I'd end up in a chocolate-induced coma, so I stopped while I was ahead.

"I've got my camera. Let's get a good picture of us all together," Vance said, pulling his photography gear out of the locker behind him. We all clustered together with Marco in the middle. All of us were squished in tightly around our instructor, grinning like maniacs, warm around the edges from the wine, pizza, and cake.

"Everyone, say 'chow.' That's how you pronounce this word on my shirt. It means 'hello' in Italian," Marco said, pointing at the letters on his faded red T-shirt with the Italian greeting *Ciao* in fancy script across the front.

"*Ciao!*" we all shouted.

"It also means 'good-bye,' but I much prefer 'hello,' don't you?" Marco said, sliding his arm around Katia's waist in a well-practiced flirtatious move.

Katia slid out of his grasp without responding and grabbed the last slice of pizza.

"Okay, students. You have finished your food? It is time for working. *Andiamo!*" said Marco. He'd had a couple of glasses of wine by now, and his English had gone downhill a little. Like Tessa, who tended to switch over to Italian whenever she was drunk or stressed.

"We will go now to the studio, and I will show you the cane-making."

Marco was here to teach us an ancient glass technique that was the first step in making beautiful millefiori beads. First, we'd make glass canes, which were slender pieces of patterned glass with flower designs running through them. Then we'd learn to use them in the torch to make beads.

"Where are you staying, Marco?" Vance asked.

Dez poured himself another glass of wine. "He's going to stay in our instructor's cottage out back, near where these gals are staying," he said, gesturing toward Lara and Sara. "It's real nice; all the comforts of home."

I'd seen the cottages when Sam showed us the field behind the shop, and to me, "real nice" didn't seem to describe them accurately. In fact, if it rained hard enough, I'd be worried about them sliding into the river a few dozen yards away.

"Are you camping?" I asked Vance, wondering where he was going to stay, since there were only two trailers.

"Oh, me? Yeah, I am. I've got my tent right here," Vance said, poking the backpack on the floor with a boot.

"You're going to stay dry in a flimsy little tent?" Tessa asked. She had to be thinking about her own unhappy girls who were camping this week. Several days of rain wouldn't improve their experience at the camp or their attitudes.

"Oh, yeah, I've got a tarp for underneath it. As long as we don't have an epic flood, I'll be fine," Vance said.

"Okay, my students, we start now," said Marco. Then turned to Sam. "Now, Stan—"

"*Sam*," he corrected.

"Right...you have shown the students the furnace?" Marco asked. Sam nodded along with everyone else. Duke, standing with his arms folded, rolled his eyes like he was too advanced to have to hear about the furnace.

"I'll put the tip of the punty into the furnace, then rotate the punty to gather some molten glass from the crucible," Marco said, picking up a long steel rod and showing it to the class. "When I bring the punty out of the furnace, I'll have a—how you say?—blob of clear glass, the size of an egg. If there is more glass than we need, I'll let it drip into this pot filled with water. It's called a crack-off bucket."

"And everyone, we only want clear glass in that bucket. We can recycle it as long as it doesn't have any color mixed in with it," Dez said from his stool at the back of the workshop, where he sat with a wine glass in his hand.

"Now, what I'm going to teach you to do is called pulling cane. A cane is a thin rod of glass, about as thick as a pencil. We start with our glass here on the punty, and we pull it out into one long cane, then we break it into short sections."

Marco opened his toolkit and rummaged around in it. He pulled out several exotic looking tools and molds before pulling out a bundle of sample canes in bubble wrap. "This is what we get if we make these canes correctly," Marco said, unwrapping the canes and showing us the ends of them, then flipping them around so we could see the same patterns on the opposite ends of each. "There is a pattern all the way through."

"It reminds me of the designs in taffy or those Christmas candies we used to buy that had pictures running through them," I said.

"I do not know these candies," Marco said as he carefully rewrapped the canes he was holding.

"Oh, right. I know what you mean," said Sam. "It's just like that—each slice has a design in it, all cut from the same long piece."

"*Si, si,* that's right. We're going to take the slices—in Italian they're called *murrine*—and we will decorate beads with them. Like a mosaic, taking all the little murrine and applying them on to the bead to create an intricate floral design," Marco explained.

"We'll have a day at my studio, Fremont Fire, to work on beads this week," Tessa said.

"Violetta will be showing us samples of the beads as soon as she gets here," said Abby, who was looking a little nervous with half of her instruction team still missing. "She'll be giving you a presentation later this week about the types of vintage Italian beads that are made with murrine. It's an ancient Italian technique, and I know she's excited to share it with you."

"I brought these from home. They belonged to my nonna," Tessa said, passing the strand of her grandmother's beads to Marco.

"These are excellent examples of old Venetian beads with the millefiori design. All the different flower patterns are murrine," Marco replied. "Thank you—Tessa, is it?"

Tessa nodded, but said nothing.

Marco passed the strand to Katia, leaning in extra close to her and pointing out the flower details.

"Perhaps you would like to model it for us?" Marco suggested to Katia, who promptly passed the necklace on to Vance, giving a clear non-verbal rejection of his idea. Katia was obviously not appreciating Marco's attention.

"Because you are new to glassblowing..." Marco started to say to the class.

"I'm not new, I've been working with glass for years," said Duke.

"Yes, of course. Good for you. Others here have not had the experience," Marco nodded to the rest of us.

Duke stood with his arms crossed, waiting for Marco to continue.

"Can you open the furnace door?" Marco asked me.

"Sure," I said, tentatively touching the handle of the furnace door. It was warm, but not too hot to touch. I slid the small door back on its rails toward me. As soon as the door was open, the heat blasted out of the furnace opening.

"Oh! You need color," Abby said, unlocking a cabinet and pulling out a pint-sized plastic container full of colored glass powder. She grabbed a pie tin, poured the powder into it, rushed to the marver, and set it down.

Marco put the tip of the punty into the furnace. Like pulling honey from a pot, he brought out a mass of clear molten glass about the size of a plum. He let a little drip into the bucket of water on the floor at his feet. As he stood next to the furnace, he rotated the punty expertly between his fingers, keeping the remaining glass on-center so that no more dripped off.

He rolled the molten mass into the pile of glass powder until it was pink all over. He repeated this process several times. After adding a layer of color, the students took turns opening the furnace door so Marco could add another layer of clear glass, followed by another layer of glass powder, until he had a glass ball the size of a grapefruit. He brought the hot glass ball over to us so we could examine it. There wasn't much to see yet, but I knew that with all the layers Marco added, the magic was on the inside of the mass of glass and would be revealed once it was cool.

"Now for the fun part," Duke said with a know-it-all tone, sure of what would come next.

"We take the diamond shears, and we grab hold of the hot glass," said Marco. Sam stepped forward with an unusual pair of scissors. The blades of the shears were notched, rather than straight, so that when the blades closed they created a diamond-shaped opening, rather than a straight edge. Marco nodded to Sam to go ahead and take the next step in the process. He grabbed the tip of the molten blob with his diamond shears, catching just enough glass in the blades to get a firm grip on the hot glass. Sam started to walk backward, pulling on the blob. It got thinner and thinner as he headed down the hallway toward the kitchen, all the while holding the tip of the glass in the diamond shears. As the blob lengthened and cooled, it became more and more difficult for him to pull on what was now a pencil-thin rod of glass.

The men put the ten-foot-long glass cane on the floor. Using a pair of tile nippers, they broke the cane into a dozen smaller pieces. Since the glass was still too hot to handle, Marco donned a leather glove and picked up a segment. He looked at one end of the glass rod, and then at the other end.

"Ah, good. You know in Italian, we say *bene*," he said, holding out the cane so we could see the end of it. The end revealed a series of concentric pink circles. He flipped the rod around so we could see the other end. "You see, the design, it goes all the way through."

"*Bene*," Tessa said.

"Good, Tessa. Everyone say it: *bene*," Marco said.

"*Bene!*" we all chimed in.

"Now each of you will try it. Do not worry. I will help you."

Duke was the first student to try making a cane. Being the most experienced, he had no trouble pulling molten glass from the furnace and adding the layers of colors. With Vance's help, he pulled several feet of cane.

"Okay, nice job," Marco said. "Who is next?"

I raised a tentative hand.

"Yes, now you will you try it," Marco said, handing me a punty and opening the small door in the furnace. As soon as the door was open, I looked into the furnace's screaming orange inferno. I reached forward with the punty, trying desperately to see into the blazing pot. It was excruciatingly hot—hotter than anything I'd ever experienced while beadmaking, or any other time for that matter.

I pulled the punty away from the furnace and took a few stumbling steps backward, nearly knocking over the bucket of water on the floor. Marco strode to my side and took the punty from me.

"It is okay. You will try again later," he said, giving me a pat on the back. While I knew Marco was trying to be supportive, I felt his attitude toward me was a bit condescending. I was embarrassed to have been such a wimp. I'd worked with molten glass for more than three years. Why was this so difficult for me? I tried not to frown as I watched the other students.

Tessa was next. While it was a little difficult for her to see into the furnace since she was not very tall, she was able to get a small gather of hot glass from the furnace and pull out a few feet of cane. She lived in Venice on and off, and while I don't think she blew glass while she was growing up, she certainly spent hundreds, if not thousands of hours watching glassblowers in studios in Italy.

When it was Katia's turn, Marco seemed to take extra time helping her, standing close behind her as she gathered glass from the furnace. Katia's thin-lipped expression made it clear she was not enjoying being the teacher's pet.

The students worked for a few hours, although I was only watching, trying to gather enough courage to try again. Marco approached me after everyone had another turn.

"Do you want to try one more time?" Marco asked.

I shook my head. "Sorry, maybe I can try tomorrow."

"Yes, you will do it tomorrow. Everyone, we are done for the day. I am going now, to drink Abby's terrible wine in the kitchen. I am hoping everyone will join me, because bad wine is better than no wine at all," Marco said, eyeing Katia. Abby grimaced, headed to her office, and slammed the door.

"Sorry, I'm out of here," Katia said, heading for the rolling door.

"Where are you staying?" Marco asked. This was more than idle chitchat; he was hoping for a little romance.

"Down at the Cascade Corners Motel. Doesn't seem too awful, if you don't mind a few roaches running for cover when you turn on the lights."

"I will walk with you," Marco offered as he reached toward Katia, trying to help her put on her coat.

"I can take care of myself," Katia said, pressing her open palm against Marco's chest, pushing him away. She grabbed her raincoat and her canvas bag and headed out the door, zipping up her coat as she slogged off into the rain.

Dez peered out the door and watched Katia walking alone

through the rain.

"I'm staying at that same motel. I'll make sure she gets there safely," Duke told Dez as he headed out the door.

"Thank you." Dez opened the kitchen cupboard, grabbed a bottle, and poured himself a hefty glass of whiskey. He moved into the studio and started cleaning up, his booze in one hand, and a cigarette hanging out of the corner of his mouth. He took the tub of powdered glass that Marco had used and returned it to the locked cabinet. I noticed that the other colors the students had been using were still sitting out.

"Do you want me to bring these colors over so you can lock them up, too?" I asked Dez.

"No, we lock up the expensive colors. That pink's got a lot of gold in it to make that vibrant color. Costs an arm and a leg," Dez said. Finished with his work, he headed for the kitchen. "I'm opening up more wine, unless someone wants something stronger."

Tessa and I left before we got roped into having wine with Dez, Marco, and any other classmates who were willing to have a drink with one guy who likely had too much alcohol in his bloodstream already and another who had too much testosterone.

FIVE

I GRABBED THE TRAY that held the cake I brought for Tessa, along with the knife and other supplies. The rain was coming down steadily now as Tessa and I jogged toward the Ladybug. Juggling the tray, I reached in my purse and grabbed my keys, fumbling to unlock the car with the key fob. I stepped in a puddle and my feet slipped in the mud. The contents of the tray, all but the cake, fortunately, slid into the bushes.

"Dammit!" I shouted. Tessa and I grabbed what we could, placed the cake and the soggy supplies in the trunk, and jumped in the car. I looked over at Tessa, sitting next to me.

"At least we were able to save the cake," Tessa said with a smile.

"True, and I think I might need another piece by the time we get home," I said.

I started the car and headed out of Carthage. The rain continued pelting down, and it was difficult to drive on the narrow road. The wipers swept across the windshield at a furious rate, but they couldn't keep ahead of the deluge. I was having second thoughts about our decision to drive each day. In fact, I was having second thoughts about taking this class at all. I'd failed at the most basic lesson—pulling hot glass out of the furnace.

"I can hear you thinking," Tessa said. "You're not a failure. Everyone learns at their own pace, especially when it comes to glass." She reached into her purse and started rummaging around inside.

"What are you looking for?" I asked.

"My phone," Tessa said, dumping the contents of her handbag in her lap. "I can't find my phone!"

"Maybe it's in a pocket or fell on the floor between the seat and the console. Here, use my phone to call yours, and we'll see if we hear it ringing." Tessa dialed her phone number and we listened. We could hear ringing in the speaker of my phone, but we couldn't hear Tessa's phone in the car.

"Oh, geez, Tessa, you took a picture of me with your phone, remember?"

"You're right. I did," Tessa said, her voice rising in panic. "I must have left it on the table in the kitchen."

The rain started coming down even harder. Gripping the steering wheel, I was determined to keep driving toward home. Tessa was quiet, too quiet, but she wouldn't stay that way for long. She couldn't live without her phone all night.

"Please don't make me turn around and get your phone. It's already late, and we're going to get home even later if we have to backtrack," I said.

"But what if one of my kids needs me?"

I didn't reply.

The silence grew. I knew I should stick to my guns and keep driving, but Tessa was much more stubborn than I was. No one, certainly not me, can say no to Tessa for long. The farther away from the studio I got, the longer it would take to get home if I acquiesced to Tessa's demands to return to Carthage. If I turned back now, at least I'd shorten the amount of backtracking I'd have to do, and I wouldn't have to deal with Tessa badgering me about her phone.

"I might as well turn around now so you can get the phone instead of nervously pacing around my house all night, wondering if someone needs you but can't get ahold of you." I flipped a not-strictly-speaking-legal U-turn.

Once we got back to the studio, I idled on Main Street while Tessa ran to the front door. She tried the door, but it was locked. She looked in the window next to the rolling door, cupping her hands against the pane. Tessa turned and ran toward me faster than I've ever seen her move, a look of horror on her face. She leapt into the car, slammed the door, and locked it.

"*Dio mio*, Jax! It's Marco, he's dead! He's lying across the marver in the hot shop, white as a ghost!"

Suddenly, the bushes that ran alongside the studio down to the river started thrashing wildly and a cloaked figure emerged from them.

"Go, go, go!" Tessa shouted, pounding on the dashboard. "That could be the murderer."

I pulled away from the curb and sped down Main Street, looking in my rearview mirror as I drove. There was no sign of the shrouded person we had seen.

"Call 911!" I said, thrusting my cell phone at Tessa.

She dialed the number and pressed the speaker button. When the emergency dispatcher answered, Tessa told him what she had seen through the window.

"Are you somewhere safe?" the dispatcher asked.

"No! We saw someone walking next to the studio—maybe the killer," Tessa shouted into the phone. I continued driving down Main Street until I reached the end of town.

"Now what am I supposed to do?" I asked, hoping either the 911 dispatcher or Tessa could give me some guidance.

"Find a safe place where you can stay until officers arrive," the dispatcher said.

The last building in Carthage was a car repair shop. I pulled up to the side of the building, between two other cars that looked like they hadn't seen the open road in a decade, judging from their lack of tires and the cinder blocks they sat on. Old Firehouse Studio was on the other side of the road from the garage and a long way down Main Street.

"I think we're somewhere safe now," I said, turning off the

Ladybug, shutting off her headlights, and making sure the doors were locked. "We're at the end of Main Street, where it meets the highway in Carthage."

"What are we supposed to do now?" Tessa asked the dispatcher.

"I've sent the sheriff a message with your location, and he is on his way. Do you want me to stay on the line with you until he arrives?" the man asked.

"No, we're okay now," Tessa said. I nodded agreement.

"Before I let you go, I need to get your contact information, in case we need to follow up with you in the future. It's standard operating procedure."

Tessa gave the dispatcher our phone numbers and hung up. We sat in the dark and waited. The rain slowed to nothing more than a trickle. Finally, a set of headlights came toward us and swept across the car. A sheriff's cruiser came to a stop next to us, completely black other than the golden six-pointed star on the driver's side door. The sheriff hoisted himself out of the cruiser and headed toward us, hitching up his pants, which had been pulled low by the heavy revolver at his waist. I rolled down my window as he approached.

"Hello there, ladies. How ya doing there?"

"We're freaked out, thank you very much!" Tessa said, her voice taut with fear and impatience. We had been waiting for at least fifteen minutes for this man to arrive. Meanwhile, who knew what was happening down at the studio. "Have you been to the studio? What's happening there?"

"Well, now, I drove by on my way to see you two girls. I didn't see anything unusual going on, and I got the coordinates from the emergency operator telling me to come here, so here I am."

"But you need to be at Old Firehouse Studio! Something horrible has happened there."

"Now, you're just fired up. I'm sure it was nothing. When I drove by it was all dark, and I didn't see anyone running around in a murderous rampage. I'm glad you girls are okay after your scare. Now, why don't you two go on home. You live around here?" the sheriff asked.

"We live in Seattle. We were headed home when I realized I forgot my phone, so we went back to get it and I saw a man we know—his dead body—through the window of the studio," Tessa said. "We called 911 and then drove here and parked."

"You two girls are obviously shaken." I cringed. This man had called us girls three times in the last thirty seconds. Both Tessa and I were on our long slow slide toward fifty, hardly girls at this point. I decided it would be in our best interest to grin and bear it. "You leave it to me, Sheriff Poole, at your service," the sheriff said, tipping his hat and simultaneously hitching up his trousers again. "You head on home, and I'll make sure to deal with whatever it is that happened down there at that glassblowing studio." He thumped the ragtop of my car with his meaty hand, a signal that we should take off. Water sprayed in every direction as his hand bounced off the fabric. Drops spattered his face. He cursed as he fumbled for a handkerchief in his back pocket and returned to his cruiser. He did not inspire confidence.

As I pulled out of the auto repair shop and turned toward the highway, the sheriff turned on his cruiser's sirens and lights and sped back toward Old Firehouse Studio.

Tessa and I didn't talk much after that. I spent most of the time concentrating on my driving and trying to figure out how to ask her the right questions.

"Are you sure you saw Marco? You are positive he was dead?"

"Yes," was all Tessa would say.

"Could it have been something else?"

"No."

"Do you need a cookie?"

"Yes."

•   •   •

When we arrived at my house, we went immediately to Val's front door, in search of a cookie for Tessa. My neighbor whipped the door open dramatically, her silky leopard-print blouse fluttering in the breeze caused by the door's swift movement.

"Oh. It's you," Val said.

"Expecting someone else?" I asked.

"Oh, yes, but, I don't want to talk about it."

"That's okay, because we desperately need a cookie, and you can tell us who you're waiting for some other time." This was a smart move, because if Val started talking about one of her boyfriends, we could be standing on her doorstep all night.

"Oh! A cookie. I can do that. I have cookies," Val said, trotting to her kitchen. She didn't invite us in.

Val grabbed a zebra-striped cookie jar and jammed it into my outstretched hands. "As always, it's faboo that you stopped by," Val said, hurriedly closing the door. She opened it again and added, "Oatmeal raisin."

"Is this your way of saying you've got someone coming over tonight?" I asked, holding the door before she could shut it again.

"No, it's my way of telling you what kind of cookie is in the jar," Val said, scooting us off the welcome mat. "Bye-bye." She shut the door. How odd. She was usually delighted to see me. In fact, I often had trouble getting Val to stop talking and leave me alone.

"I wonder who she's waiting for," Tessa said.

"I'll find out eventually. She always has trouble keeping her secrets from me, or anyone else, for very long." On my side of the duplex, Tessa and I settled onto the sofa.

"Cookie?" I opened the jar and offered Tessa one.

"Thanks," Tessa said, taking a bite.

"We need milk. We've got to have milk," I said, finding the carton in the refrigerator and filling two glasses. As soon as Gumdrop heard the fridge door open, he was next to me, spinning between my legs and looking up at me with those big green eyes.

"Did Val come over and feed you?" My cat wasn't going to say one way or another. If someone was willing to feed him, that was perfectly all right with him, even if he'd already eaten. I popped open a can of Gummie's favorite Savory Salmon and plopped a couple of heaping tablespoons into his dish. For once, he didn't just smell the food and walk away. He actually started eating it. The poor guy was really hungry.

I handed my friend a glass of milk and settled back down next to her. "Tessa, are you okay?" I asked. She looked as pale as the glass of milk she was holding. "Is it Marco? You have every right to be upset about him. It's dreadful to have seen what you did."

"It's just that …" Tessa choked up and shook her head. She couldn't continue.

"It's okay. Everything is going to be fine. The sheriff said he's going to take care of everything."

"I miss my kids and Craig, especially since this disturbing thing with Marco happened."

"I know. It's horrible. You've got me this week. I'll be your support, okay?" I said.

"You're my support every week," Tessa said, giving me a hug. "What do you think is going to happen with class?"

"I guess that's something Dez and Abby are going to have to figure out. They'll have to find another teacher, or refund everyone's money, or reschedule, I guess," I said.

"It's impossible to reschedule when the teacher is not coming back…to life," Tessa said.

"Another cookie?"

"Not even a cookie can help with this mess."

SIX

THE NEXT MORNING I woke up with broiling feet. It was Gumdrop's fault. Fortunately, I had trained him to stop sleeping on my head, but sleeping on my feet wasn't much better. It made it hard to roll over, and I woke up feeling like I'd been wearing slippers all night. Gumdrop looked like a pair of fluffy gray slippers, so in my groggy, pre-caffeinated brain it seemed to make sense.

I padded down the hallway, Gumdrop at my heels, and made some coffee. There was no sign of Tessa. After the coffee finished brewing, Tessa still hadn't appeared, and that was strange. Usually the smell of coffee would bring her running.

I tapped on the door of the guest room. "Tessa? Are you okay? Do you want coffee?"

"Ugh."

"Are you all right?"

"Too…many…cookies…"

"We shouldn't have eaten the whole jar. But, that was last night, and my mom always says you shouldn't dwell on the past," I said through the door.

"Ugh." She opened the door a crack. "Is there coffee?" she asked weakly.

"Of course. I can't believe you didn't smell it through the door."

"I think I'm in sensory overload. Too much oatmeal, too many raisins. Aren't those things supposed to be healthy?"

"It's the sugar that holds them together that might be the problem."

Tessa shuffled out to the big oak table in the kitchen.

"Here you go," I said, shoveling two heaping spoons of sugar into the cup, giving it a swift stir, and handing her the mug. "I bet you're going to skip breakfast."

"Ugh."

"That's what I thought."

After half a mug of coffee, Tessa was starting to perk up. "I'm going to take a shower. We should probably get out to the studio before too long," Tessa said.

"I wonder what it'll be like out there today."

"Probably a zoo with police and reporters everywhere. I'm calling Abby," I said.

I called Old Firehouse Studio and Sam answered.

"Sam! Thank God I reached you. What's happening out there?"

"No one else is here yet. Are you on your way?" he asked.

"Everything's fine?"

"Uh, yeah. I'm going to start up the kilns in the hot shop."

"No cops? No reporters?"

"Noooo. Should there be?"

"Okay, thanks. Tessa and I will be there soon." I decided to wait until we arrived at the studio to see for myself what was happening, before telling Sam what Tessa had seen last night. When Tessa was dressed, I gave her an update, telling her Sam seemed to think everything at the studio was fine.

"Or maybe he's clueless and hasn't talked with Abby or the police yet. Don't tell me Marco is alive and well. I know what I saw," Tessa said, taking a sip of her second cup of coffee and giving me one of her fiercest glares.

"Let's get out there and find out what happened. What are we waiting for?"

"For the coffee to kick in," Tessa replied.

• • •

When we arrived at the studio, everything was oddly normal. We parked and went inside. The studio was empty. I hated to look into the hot shop, afraid of what I might see. I forced myself to glance over, but there was no dead body. Had we dreamed Tessa had seen a corpse? Was I now in a cookie-binge induced daze, imagining a scene in which a dead man had tidily cleaned himself up and walked away?

I found Abby in her office.

"Hey, Jax. How are you this morning?"

"Oh my God, Abby, the real question is how are you? How terrible…"

"Oh, we're okay, Dez and I, we're always fighting. It happens after being married for all these years."

"No, I mean, you know, with Marco."

"Marco? Oh, I haven't seen him yet today," Abby said. "Probably still jet-lagged and sleeping in."

"Because Tessa saw Marco, and he was—"

"Drunk?"

"No. Dead."

"What? That's crazy. He was probably out drinking last night with Dez."

"Where's Dez now? Maybe he saw what happened last night."

"I haven't seen Dez all night. You know, he and I get mad at each other, and he goes off drinking and disappears, sometimes for a couple of days. He'll be back, hung over and apologetic later today. It'll be fine. Are you sure it wasn't you two who were out drinking last night? Seeing things in the dark?"

Although we were hung over this morning, it was from too many oatmeal cookies, not too much alcohol. Tessa joined us in Abby's office.

"Abby, I swear, last night I saw Marco, and he was dead," Tessa said, pulling Abby from her chair and marching her to the hot shop. "Right there, lying across the marver. Dead!"

"I think you might have seen me charging the furnace," Sam said, coming in from the utility yard. "I fill it with these fifty pound bags of crushed glass and I set a few on the marver last night. Maybe you saw those? When the lights are off and the furnace is glowing, it casts some pretty weird shadows."

"Look, I know what I saw. I don't want you to tell me I saw shadows or bags of glass. I saw Marco and he was dead. His eyes were open—so was his mouth—his arms were pale and flung out on either side of his motionless body."

"Let's go find Marco, and I can prove to you he's not dead. Okay? Oh, and here's your phone. I found it in the kitchen after you left last night," Abby said, handing Tessa her cell phone.

We followed Abby as she huffed down the steps to the field, convinced that once we saw Marco alive and well, the argument would be over. For our part, Tessa and I were convinced that once Abby saw Marco was missing, she'd be ready to believe something horrible had happened last night.

Abby banged on the trailer door. "Marco! You in there? Marco!" There was no answer. She twisted the doorknob and the door swung open. Not a soul was there.

"Maybe Marco went out for some breakfast," Abby said, refusing to believe her instructor was gone for good.

"How can we find Dez?" I asked. "Maybe he saw something."

"When Dez goes on a bender, we might not see him for a couple of days. Who knows which bar he'd be at," Abby said. "I'm not worried about him. It happens all the time."

The Twins stumbled out of their trailer about fifty feet from where we were standing.

"Are we starting class early?" they asked. I barely recognized them with no make-up and in their matching black footie pajamas. I would never have guessed they were the long john type.

Farther down the slope toward the river, Vance's tent was barely standing. It looked like it had flooded all night long. Hearing the commotion, he pulled himself out of the tent. He was sopping wet.

"Vance!" I said, running through the soggy field to him. "Are you okay?"

"*Ah-choo!*" Vance let rip the biggest sneeze I'd ever heard. It nearly bowled me over.

"Oh, Vance, come on, let's get you inside," Tessa said, her maternal instincts taking over. "Maybe I can make you some tea."

Vance, Tessa, and I sloshed through the field, with Sam and Abby bringing up the rear.

"Stand here, dude, next to the furnace. It will dry you out and warm you up," Sam told Vance, once we were back inside. Tessa brought Vance a cup of tea and stood with him next to the furnace, trying to warm up as well.

Since I was cold and wet, too, I slid up next to Tessa and Vance, trying to get a sliver of the heat radiating from the furnace. The crack-off bucket was right in front of the furnace, so I dragged it a few feet to get it out of the way. The glass shards in the bottom of the pot glistened as the water sloshed from side to side.

"Did anything weird happen last night after we left?" I asked Vance.

"What kind of weird are we talking about?"

"We can't find Marco this morning. Did you see him last night after we all went our separate ways?"

"No, I bundled up in my tent and tried to stay warm and dry. That wasn't easy. I sure hope it doesn't rain again tonight."

"Were you out of your tent at all last night?" I was wondering if he'd seen anyone, or if it had been him we'd seen in the bushes at the side of the building.

"I went out at one point to use the bathroom. I was going to use the studio's john, but the doors were locked. I ended up going by the river, but it was hard getting down there through all those bushes."

"You didn't see anything going on in the studio when you were up?"

"No, not a thing. I didn't have my glasses on, so unless it was the size of a rhinoceros, I might not even have noticed it. Wait, come to think of it, I did see something. I saw a car speeding away from the studio."

It was likely Vance had seen Tessa and me driving away last night. Or perhaps he'd seen someone else, like the murderer, making a quick getaway.

"Really? Do you know what kind of car it was?" I asked.

"Sorry, I couldn't see much of anything in the dark."

Abby picked up the studio phone. "I'll call Dez. Maybe he's crawled home by now and he can tell me what the hell is going on. Oh, wait. I have a message." She listened to the message, then dialed her phone.

"Hey, Harvey. I got your message. Sorry you had to come out last night in the rain. You'd better get out here. We think our instructor might be missing," Abby said. Tessa looked hard at Abby with big bulging eyes, "or dead," Abby added with Tessa's non-verbal encouragement. "Oh, and we can't find Dez either. Can you hit some of the local places?"

Abby hung up. "The sheriff said he'd be out as soon as he's finished breakfast and told me he'd stop at some of the bars Dez likes on his way over."

"The sheriff didn't see anything when he came out last night?" I asked.

"He said he showed up, no one was here, everything was locked up. No dead bodies. Nothing. He talked with a couple of women—must have been you two. He left me a message here last night. That's the message I just heard." Abby called the others in from the break room. "We're going to start class a little later than planned," Abby said. "We need to track down Marco and Dez, and then we'll get started."

"Why doesn't everyone come with me and we can look at what we made last night, now that it's all cooled down," Sam said, opening one of the kilns and looking inside.

"Tessa and I'll go out and get some pastries. That'll help the situation," I said. Pastries helped a lot of situations, but I didn't think it would help us solve how a dead body could appear and then disappear into thin air. "We'll bring back enough for everyone." I figured a few carbs and a little caffeine could help all of us.

Abby mouthed the words thank you, and pressed her palms together in mock prayer, as we headed out the door.

"Wasn't there a diner down here somewhere?"

"Yes, it's about the only thing in town other than the studio and the car repair shop. Maybe if we're lucky, we'll find Dez and Marco there having breakfast."

"You know it's not possible," Tessa said, shaking her head.

"Of course I do. I don't know if you noticed, but Marco's bed was made. He didn't sleep in it last night."

"That's because he never made it back to his trailer."

"You mean cottage," I said with a smirk.

Tessa responded by playfully smacking me on the arm.

We walked down Main Street and a few minutes later arrived at the Robin's Nest Café. It was utterly still inside the restaurant. A man in his fifties stood behind the cash register looking smart and trim in a clean white oxford shirt with a red apron over the top of some well-creased khakis.

"Hi there, lovely ladies! May I get you a table?" the man asked with a bright toothpaste-commercial smile, putting down his paper to greet us.

"No, thanks. We'd like two of your largest coffees and a box of donuts. Do you have any?"

"No donuts, but, you're in luck," said the owner, "We have muffins, even better than donuts."

"We'd like two dozen," Tessa said, handing the man her credit card.

"All of them? That never happens around here," said the man, chuckling. "We don't get many visitors. Is this your first time in Carthage?"

"It is," I said. And probably my last, but I wasn't going to say it out loud.

"Vickie!" The man hollered over his shoulder. "Can you bring out all the muffins? We've got some takers."

Minutes later, a woman came bustling out of the kitchen carrying two rectangular pink boxes.

"That's my wife, Vickie. She's my cook. She makes the best muffins in town," the man said.

The only muffins in town, I thought. Vickie set the muffin boxes down on the counter in front of us.

"And I'm Carl, the owner of this fine establishment. Here are your muffins. I was looking forward to sneaking one of them later, but you get them instead," he said, patting his flat belly. "That's the good news."

"Maybe I'll make more." Vickie slumped onto the stool behind the counter. The dark shadows beneath her eyes told me she was exhausted, but not simply from a poor night's sleep. Instead, it was clear her exhaustion went much deeper, caused by years of hard work or heartache. "Enjoy the muffins. They're chocolate chip. I make a different kind each day, so check back tomorrow," she said, rubbing her neck and trying to smile.

"Thanks," Tessa said, retrieving her credit card, then reaching over the counter and grabbing a box and a cup of coffee. I did the same.

•   •   •

Tessa and I walked slowly down the street back to the glass studio.

"I know what I saw last night was real. Marco is dead, Jax," said Tessa. "As for Dez, I'm a little worried about what has happened to him, too."

"You think he could've killed Marco?" I asked.

"Or he was killed by the same person who killed Marco."

"What do you think we should do?"

"I think we should wait until the sheriff gets here. Maybe he'll be able to tell us what he's found out about Dez. Maybe he'll have been at a bar, and we can stop worrying about him."

"And Dez can tell us what happened last night with Marco. But if Dez was the culprit, I bet we'll never see him again," I said.

We slurped down the rest of our coffee and tossed the cups in the can by the front door of the studio.

"We've got muffins," Tessa said as we entered the kitchen. Vance was tinkering with the coffee maker while the Twins sat at the table with a dozen packets of black Swarovski crystal beads, stringing them into long strands along with some of their own handmade glass beads, which were shaped like crimson spiders and ivory skulls.

"We'll have coffee any minute. I think I've finally got it working," Vance said, plugging in the Mr. Coffee and flipping the switch.

Everyone gathered in the kitchen while Tessa and I passed around the muffins.

"Unfortunately, until we find Marco de Luca, we're going to have to postpone class. When we find him, we'll call you. Make sure I have a cell number for you," Abby said.

I didn't think there was any chance of finding Marco alive, if we were able to find him at all. It seemed to me that whoever killed him had succeeded in cleaning up and hiding the body. Somehow, I doubted we'd see Dez again, because he was either on the run after killing Marco, or worse, he was also dead.

Clearly angry that the class had been delayed, Duke headed for the door. A tall dark-haired woman stood in the doorway, hands on her hips.

"Where is Marco?" she asked, as Duke barged past her.

SEVEN

"**VIOLETTA!** What are you doing here?" Abby asked. "I didn't think you were getting in until later today."

"I used a little persuasion to get on a flight that hadn't left yet. It was delayed, like me, and they let me trade my ticket in," Violetta said.

"When did you get here? Did you take a shuttle?" Abby asked.

"Last night, very late, in that terrible storm. I rented a car and found my way out to this awful little motel. What is it? Cascade Corners? It's not a nice place. Only disgusting people would stay there."

Katia gave Violetta an indignant glare.

Violetta was beautiful in a severe Italian way, with sharp features and short, stylish hair, right off a Milan runway. While Val wouldn't approve of Violetta's harshness, she would definitely approve of her fashion sense and style.

"Where is Marco? It is time for the start of class," said Violetta, checking the gold watch on her slender wrist.

"We don't know where he is right now," Abby said. I couldn't believe how fervently Abby wanted to believe Marco was going to walk in the door at any moment.

"Tsk, Marco, he's always mad at me for being late, and now here he is not even ready for class. He's probably with some woman, so typical of him," said Violetta. She spotted Katia. "You, you spent time with Marco last night?" Violetta asked.

Katia glared fiercely at Violetta, who had, in the span of thirty seconds, offended her by insulting her choice of hotels and making assumptions about her choice of sleeping partners.

"I'll have you know, I did not take Marco up on his offer to walk me home," Katia said stiffly.

"He must have found someone else. He's not picky," Violetta said, infuriating Katia even more.

"Have you been in touch with Marco since you arrived?" Abby asked.

"No. I didn't want to call him so late last night. Besides, I didn't want to interrupt him while he was taking advantage of some hot glass girl who had her sights set on a superstar glass artist twice her age."

•   •   •

Sheriff Poole showed up a few minutes later. He nodded at Tessa and me, acknowledging he remembered us from the night before.

"I drove past the two local bars, but they weren't open yet. There weren't any cars parked in the lots, but I can stop back by around happy hour," the sheriff said. It occurred to me he might be stopping by because he was going to take advantage of the happy hour drink specials, but I decided to give him the benefit of the doubt.

"Sheriff, there was most definitely a dead body here last night. My friend Tessa is not making this up," I said, walking into the hot shop. "Shouldn't this be a crime scene?"

"Well, little lady," the sheriff said. "I don't see any crime to turn into a scene. I came over after I talked with you girls last night and the place was quiet. You must've imagined seeing something in the dark. It happens in unfamiliar territory, but it was nothing to worry about. I suggest you all go back to having your class, and I'll keep looking for Dez."

"I saw a corpse in this studio!" Tessa said, nearly vibrating with frustration because no one seemed to be listening to us. "How do you explain the fact that two people are missing?"

"Well, now, if you were from around here, which you are not, you'd know our buddy Dez, he likes to drink a little bit. He can disappear for a couple of days sometimes and no one worries about him. Isn't that right, Abby?" Abby nodded and grimaced. Even if this was typical, I'm sure Abby still worried about her husband when he went AWOL for days at a time. "What we've got here are two men on a drinking spree, until further notice."

"But what if they're not? You've got no proof they're even together, let alone alive," I said.

"See, here's the thing. We can't call this a homicide. There's no body to examine. No body, no crime."

"I'm pretty sure that's not true," I said. I could think of plenty of gangsters who were thrown off bridges with concrete shoes, and while their bodies were never recovered, there most certainly had been a crime committed. "Someone should at least look for evidence that a murder occurred. Even without a body, a detective can—"

"We don't have a detective out here, but I can do a respectable job investigating. When you figure out what I need to investigate, you let me know."

"Want a muffin?" Abby asked, offering one to the sheriff. "Did everyone else get a muffin?"

As Harvey pawed through the box, I could see why Abby wanted to make sure we'd all had one. After he had all he wanted, the box would be empty.

"I know everyone has gotten all ruffled up and confused about whatever it was that happened here," the sheriff said. "We'll start searching for this guy—"

"Guys—plural," Tessa said.

"Right. Two guys. So, in the meantime you all should keep your eyes peeled for the dead guys," the sheriff said, holding back a grin. Tessa and I were not amused.

"I wish I had seen a dead body," Lara, or possibly Sara, said.

"Yes, so macabre. So gruesome," said the other.

"Have either of you ever seen a real dead body?" Tessa asked the women.

"We like to watch horror films, the more disgusting the better," said the first. The second nodded in agreement. "Last week we saw one with zombies who were eating all these people—"

"But it wasn't as grisly as the film with the killer poodles," the other added, with a wicked smile.

"But that's not *real*. You get that, right?" Tessa asked. The fact these two dim-witted Goth chicks couldn't seem to understand the difference between fictional movie gore and real life murder was sending Tessa off the deep end.

"Whatever," they replied in unison. Tessa stood there, quietly simmering.

"I'll take one of these for the road," Sheriff Poole said, grabbing another muffin, to add to the one he had in his other hand. "And if I see either of your dead guys, I'll be in touch." The sheriff sauntered out the door, clearly with no intention of investigating. More than likely, he was going to sit behind the Robin's Nest Café in his speed trap and eat his muffins.

Duke returned to the kitchen after having stormed off. He stood at the edge of the group, looking like Gumdrop often did, his gray eyebrows furrowed in disgust. Finally, he spoke up.

"What kind of amateurish place are you running here, Abby?" Duke asked. "Your instructor's a no-show. No class today? What a waste of my time. I could be back in my own studio making things to sell."

"Listen, we'll get things back on track in no time. In the meantime, do you want to blow some glass here?" Abby asked Duke. "How about this? You can keep whatever you make."

Duke grumbled and nodded. "Okay, seems fair. I'll need an assistant." He scanned the room, looking at each of us with disapproval. "Where's Sam?"

"Sam!" Abby yelled. Moments later Sam came in from the

utility yard.

"Starting to rain again," Sam said. "You need me?"

"I need you to assist me. You get to be my punty boy," Duke said.

"Is that a thing? Sounds obscene," I whispered to Tessa. The two men started to consult with each other on what they were going to make as we followed them into the hot shop.

"It means Sam is going to be helping out Duke. He's going to do some of the work with the punty. You remember that long rod for holding hot glass? Sam will bring Duke some bits of molten glass on the end of the punty. Get your mind out of the gutter," Tessa said.

Sam took a punty over to the furnace. Katia ran to his side and opened the small door. The light from inside the furnace burst out through the opening as she slid the door open. Standing a couple of feet away from the furnace, Sam slid the punty into the molten glass within and brought out a walnut-sized blob of glass. A little molten glass dripped off the blob and hit the floor. Sam kicked it aside with this work boot.

"You call that a gather of glass? It's puny! Try again," Duke said, examining the hot glass Sam had brought him.

"You don't need to be such a jerk—"

"I thought you knew how to blow glass after all these years. If Dez were here, he'd know what to do," Duke said, not backing down.

"Guys, guys, there's no need to get angry. Sam, why don't you help Violetta get her things from the motel. I'm sure she has a lot of beads she needs to bring in," Abby said.

Sam took the punty and thrust it into a bucket of cold water. The clear glass crackled and began to break away from the shock of being cooled so quickly. Then he calmly headed out the door with Violetta right behind him.

"I guess I'm going to have to pick a helper from one of you," Duke said. I wouldn't have been surprised if he had said "one of you losers." He was eyeing Vance, who was as inexperienced as I was.

Katia stepped forward.

"I'm sure I can handle whatever you need," she said in an even, firm tone. She didn't want to be taken lightly.

"You'll do," Duke said, although what he really thought was likely the opposite.

Katia went to work gathering glass for Duke, and they seemed to work together well. Glassblowers and their assistants communicate in subtle ways: nods, hand gestures, and short words like "stop." The assistant is supposed to anticipate the glassblower's every request. It was like watching a surgeon and a nurse: scalpel, forceps, sponge—or, in this case, various glassblowing tools: punty, shears, tweezers.

Duke was sitting at the glassblower's bench rolling the blowpipe back and forth on a set of dual rails that ran on each side of the bench. Katia handed tools to him as he needed them, using wooden paddles to shield his hands from the intense heat rising from the glass vase he was making. When the piece got too cold, she reheated it in the glory hole, a cylindrical bucket-o-fire set on its side. Holding the punty, Katia thrust the piece into the glory hole to heat it to the point that it was pliable enough to work with.

Katia was doing a good job for Duke, and we watched as she competently passed the blowpipe back to him after reheating the piece.

Violetta and Sam returned and were setting up the beads in the break room, so Tessa and I wandered in to see what she had brought. I was certain Tessa was hoping to snag the best beads before anyone else could. Although I wasn't as aggressive as she was in my mission to buy beads, I was curious.

Duke shouted my name from the hot shop. I ran from the kitchen and skidded to a stop a few feet from Duke and Katia.

"Jacks!" Duke was yelling at Katia.

"Uh, did you want me?" I asked.

"What? No! What I want is for Katia to get me my large jacks!" Glassblowers use jacks, a tool that looks like a pair of giant tweezers, to create a groove in the glass before removing it from the blowpipe.

"Oh, sorry. I thought you said Jax," I said, backing out of the way while Duke continued to rotate the hot glass vase in front of him. Katia rummaged around in a bucket of equipment, finally found the large jacks, and handed the tool to Duke.

"Finally!" Duke said, yanking it out of her hands. "Now the piece is too cool. Reheat." Katia did as she was told, a look of stern determination on her face. She was handling his poor treatment well, much better than I would have been able to do in the same situation.

Violetta entered the studio. "Anyone who wishes to view the antique Venetian beads I brought with me, they are ready now," she said.

We all gathered around her magnificent display of antique Venetian beads on the break room table. The entire table was covered in strands of beads in every color of the rainbow, and in all of the traditional Italian styles. The ones we were most interested in were the millefiori beads, since they were what we were making in class. But other than those, there were some spectacular examples of beads with silver and gold foil, wedding cake beads, red and blue chevrons, and sparkling hollow orbs. Each of us took a seat and gazed in awe at the fascinating treasures before us.

"As you can see in this strand, the designs are particular to the Venetian style. And here you can see the different complicated flower patterns that create the millefiori design," Violetta said.

"Wow, some of these colors are amazing," I said, picking up a short strand in olive and purple tones.

"Yes, those are very beautiful and rare," said Violetta. "I have put a good price on those. They are much more valuable than I am asking for them." I flipped over the price tag. The strand of seven beads, a large centerpiece and six more in gradually smaller sizes, was four hundred dollars. *Four hundred dollars.*

I gently placed the beads back down on the table. Too rich for my blood.

• • •

At noon, Tessa suggested we find a place to eat for lunch.

"Do you want to try to find Meat and Eat?" I asked.

"Sure. Who wants to come with us?" Tessa asked the other students.

"We'll come," Sara and Lara said. "We've got nothing better to do."

"Sure," Vance said. "Katia and Duke told me they want to keep working. I'll ask them if they want me to bring them back anything."

A few minutes later, Vance had Katia and Duke's lunch orders, and we were off to find Meat and Eat. Vance and the Twins followed us in his car, while Tessa gave me directions using the map on her phone.

Meat and Eat was a funky old building filled with picnic tables that had red and white checked vinyl tablecloths stapled to them. The floor was covered in peanut shells, with baskets of nuts ready to eat in the middle of each table. There were exactly three sandwiches on the menu: meat, meat and cheese, and cheese. I assumed the last one was a recent addition given the growing number of vegetarians in the region.

As we waited for our lunches, Tessa and I chatted with Vance and the Twins. I asked Vance why he was taking this class.

"I want to get into glassblowing more. I like making beads, but I think some of my designs would look cool in a larger size. We'll see how I like it. I'm keeping an open mind. What about you?" he asked me.

"Geez, I guess I always want to learn new things. I'm not sure how I'm going to use the techniques. Heck, I'm not even sure I'll ever be able to master anything in the hot shop, but I love taking classes, and when Tessa told me about this one, I said yes."

"What about you two?" Vance asked the Twins.

"We want to convey our ephemeral existence with a full meta-vocabulary," one twin said.

"You basically want to be able to make different things to express yourselves?" Tessa asked.

The Twins nodded in agreement. Kudos to Tessa for being able to decipher what they said.

A restaurant employee at the pickup window called our order number, and Vance retrieved our food. He brought a stack of napkins, along with the largest submarine sandwiches I'd ever seen. Each hoagie must have been five inches tall.

"How am I supposed to eat this?" Tessa asked.

"Food is like art, sometimes it requires deconstruction," one twin said, pulling the top of the sandwich off, along with half its contents, creating an open-faced sandwich. She passed the top half to her friend and started eating what she had left.

All of us followed her lead.

"Why do you think Duke is taking this class?" I asked, between bites of sandwich. "It seems like he has a lot of experience. He wouldn't need a class to learn these techniques."

"He said it was time for him to learn some new tricks and get out of a rut. He thought some new work might sell better," Vance said.

"That makes sense," Tessa said. "I've done that before when I needed inspiration."

I hoped that was Duke's reason for being in class, and not something more sinister that had led to the demise of Dez or Marco.

EIGHT

LATE THAT AFTERNOON, I swung into the long narrow driveway between my place and the house of Mr. Chu, my cat-obsessed neighbor. He was sitting on his back porch with three cats on his lap, stroking a Persian longhair next to him. He reluctantly waved as we headed inside my house, but only after I waved at him. Mr. Chu liked cats more than humans.

"We need to get our minds off all of the bewildering things that have happened today," Tessa said.

"Like the disappearing guys," I said.

"Or the dead ones."

"Dez is in some bar, if we're to believe Abby." I knew how Abby felt, helpless and uncertain, not knowing where her partner was. I'd certainly felt that way many times when my then-boyfriend Jerry didn't come home until long after I had gone to bed, back in the days when I lived in Miami.

"I don't know what to believe, but we're never going to figure out what happened by sitting here and coming up with theories," Tessa said.

"I don't think the sheriff is going to be much help," I told her. "He doesn't seem to think anything has happened. Frankly, he wouldn't know what to do in a murder investigation if Marco's body—"

"Or Dez's—"

"Or both, showed up in a morgue."

"Maybe you should call Detective Grant," Tessa said.

"Oh no, that's not a good idea. He'll ask me out if I call him."

"And that's a problem?"

"I've been avoiding him. I don't know why, Tessa, I'm not sure I want to date a cop."

"He's not really a cop, right? He's a detective."

"He's a homicide detective," I said. "He carries a gun. He has a badge."

"You're right, he is a cop, but he doesn't get shot at much, I bet. Still, you might want to call him. Maybe you can say this is strictly business and you'll talk about a date another time."

"And…well, I worry he'll go back into his prickly mode if he's working on a murder case with me around. He wasn't the nicest guy when we were dealing with the murder at Rosie's store." I shivered. Even though a year had passed, I still had grim memories of opening the Dumpster behind Aztec Beads and discovering the body of a young woman. On that dreadful day, I also met Zachary Grant, a homicide detective for the Seattle Police Department. With his ugly tie, slicked-back old-school haircut, and steely attitude, he was the last man on earth I thought I'd be interested in, let alone who would be interested in me. But after the investigation, he warmed up to me, and I saw a kinder, gentler side of him I'd not seen before.

"He knows you better now," Tessa said, handing me the phone. Once again, no one, especially me, could say no to Tessa for long.

I tapped Zachary's name on my phone.

"Grant," the detective said in his usual serious tone. He must've looked down at that moment and spotted my name on the caller ID. "Jax, I didn't see it was you." His voice warmed as he spoke.

"Hi, Zachary," I said. I felt awkward calling him by such a formal name. I wanted to call him Zach, but he much preferred his full name. "I'm calling because, well, there's been a murder."

"I usually know about murders when they happen here in Seattle.

I haven't heard about any new incidents."

"That's because it happened in Carthage."

"Carthage? Why would you be out there mixed up with a murder?"

"Tessa and I are taking a glassblowing class. She saw a dead body through the window of the studio late last night. It was awful."

"I assume the local law enforcement is taking care of this," Zachary said, a tinge of impatience in his voice.

"The sheriff doesn't seem to think there was a murder, so I guess that's why I'm calling you, to see if there's anything you can do to help."

"Where's the body? Once a coroner gets it, the gears will start moving."

"We can't find it. Tessa saw it last night. By the time the sheriff got there, it was gone. Someone had cleaned up. No body. No blood. Nothing."

"Maybe Tessa didn't see what she thought she did."

"She really did see him. We don't know what happened after that. Oh, and the weird thing is, we don't know where one of the studio owners is, either."

"No one's worried about him?"

"No. Apparently, he goes on drinking binges and disappears for days at a time. His wife isn't particularly worried about him, at least, not yet."

"You called the police last night when Tessa saw whatever it was she saw? Did you wait for them to arrive?"

"We heard someone crashing around in the bushes outside the studio. We didn't know what else to do so we drove away and then called 911. We hid in the Ladybug behind a car repair shop until a sheriff came by, and he sent us home. But apparently, when he got to the studio, everything seemed fine to him, not a soul around, dead or alive."

"Who is it Tessa thinks she saw?"

"Marco de Luca, but she doesn't *think* she saw him. She actually saw him lying dead in the studio. He's Italian, famous in the glass world, and, well, sort of a ladies' man. He is, or was, the instructor for the class we're taking."

"Maybe he found someone to spend the night with and simply hasn't made it back yet. It's possible, right?"

"No! I believe Tessa. And get this, the sheriff said if there's no body, there's no crime."

"That's ridiculous," Zachary said. "But there needs to be some evidence that a crime was committed."

"That's what we thought. The sheriff said we'd need to find him a body before he'd start an investigation."

"He wasn't going out to look for the men or gather evidence?"

"He said he would start looking for the missing men, but I think for him that meant checking out the local bars. He's too busy manning his speed trap, and eating donuts—"

"Muffins," Tessa corrected.

"Whatever," I said, shushing her.

"You know I can't show up there and start investigating," Zachary said.

"I figured. So, we need to sit tight and wait for something else to happen? Like another murder?"

"Or for these men to come back from their drinking spree."

"But—"

"If they don't show up tomorrow, call me."

I didn't say a word.

"Put Tessa on the phone, will you? I know she's standing there."

I handed the phone to Tessa. She listened briefly and hung up.

"Well?"

"He said you shouldn't go looking for dead bodies," Tessa said. Detective Grant's surly attitude had returned, and it was aimed at me.

"Of course I won't!" I said, but I knew it was a lie. And so did Tessa.

NINE

IN THE MORNING I rolled over to find Gumdrop staring at me with his big green eyes.

"Oh! Gummie, you scared me to death." I grabbed the cat around his fat gray belly and lugged him out to the kitchen. "I'm putting you on a diet."

Gumdrop's bowl was full of crunchy food.

"Too early in the morning for catnip," I said, setting him down next to his bowl and giving him a little scratch on the chin. He closed his eyes and purred. As soon as I stopped scratching, his eyes were open and staring at me again. Ignoring him, I busied myself in the kitchen, making coffee and toast. Tessa shuffled out a few minutes later and I handed her a full cup.

"Are we headed out to Carthage?" Tessa asked.

"I got a text from Abby saying class was still canceled."

"If that's the case, I've got a question," Tessa said. "Why are you getting ready to leave?"

"Because we're going out to Carthage anyway."

"Even though there's no class?"

"There's something I want to check out."

Tessa sat in my favorite paisley wingback chair and watched as

I pulled my waterproof boots out of the closet and put them by the back door.

"That's exactly what Detective Grant did not want you to do," Tessa said.

"I don't know what you mean. I'm just taking out my boots. It's supposed to rain."

"And you're not going to use them to slog around by the river next to the studio?"

"Oh, no. I wouldn't do that."

"You have always been a rotten liar. I remember how our first grade teacher, Mrs. Martinez, wanted to know who let the hamster out of his cage. I knew it was you." Tessa and I had been friends since kindergarten. Although we spent some years apart when she lived in Italy and Seattle while I stayed in Miami, I've always considered her my best friend. There were some long stretches when we weren't in touch, when the demands of life and work got in the way of staying connected. But even though I wasn't in contact much in the years prior to my move to Seattle, Tessa and her family were at least part of the reason I came.

"I told her it was a jail break. You don't think she believed me?"

"No one believed you," Tessa said with a shake of her head, returning to the kitchen to refill her coffee cup.

"I'll only use those boots if absolutely necessary."

"You're going to look for Marco's body, aren't you? That's why we're up so early."

"I thought about it all night. You saw Marco. He was dead. He's out there rotting in Carthage somewhere. Don't you think his family would want to know where he was?"

"His parents never seemed to care where he was..." Tessa said, and then realizing she'd said something she shouldn't have, clapped a hand over her mouth.

"What did you say?"

"I meant that his parents may not care where he is," she said, back-pedaling.

"But that's not what you said. You said 'never seemed to care,' which sounds like you knew Marco's parents."

"Oh, well, I...Venice is a small city, everyone's heard of the de Luca family," Tessa said.

"Come on, you might as well spill the beans, or maybe it's *spill the beads*? I'll find out some other way."

"Okay, okay."

"I want to hear it. All of it," I said, sitting down on the sofa across from her and looking her straight in the eye.

"It's complicated."

"Don't give me that B.S. Let's start with the most basic question: Did you know Marco de Luca before yesterday?"

"It's very complicated," she said.

"And when were you planning on telling me this? And why is this the first time you've mentioned this to me. You've had many opportunities."

"It's very, very complicated."

"Let me try one more time. The man who taught the class at Old Firehouse Studio—who is likely dead, if you saw what you think you did—have you ever seen him before in your life?"

"Yes," she said, nearly whispering. "Look, my parents, they wanted me to marry a de Luca."

"What? How come I don't know about this? You were supposed to marry Marco?" I asked.

"Marco, no. Dario, his younger brother. But I chose Craig. He wasn't Venetian, not even Italian! My parents disapproved, so did my grandparents. It took them a long time to realize love trounces fame any day of the week," Tessa said. "It didn't end well with Dario."

"Wow, your parents must have been pissed at you."

"At first they didn't understand. How could I not want to be part of the famous de Luca family? They owned a giant glassblowing studio and were a big deal in the glass industry in Venice for the longest time. They made everything: vases, sculptures, chandeliers, beads. It was my grandfather, my nonno, he wanted me to marry well. He always said our family came from royalty. He like to joke that my mother named me Tessa because it was short for Contessa."

"But didn't Marco recognize you the other night?"

"Maybe. He called me Tessa. I'm not sure how he would have known my name otherwise, unless Abby told him. By the time I was with Dario—"

"With Dario? What do you mean *with*?"

Tessa ignored my question and kept going. "Marco left Venice and was traveling the world, teaching classes and exhibiting. His parents never did know where he was and didn't seem to care."

"Or, cared very deeply, but didn't know how to express it."

"Oh, they knew how to express a lot of things, trust me, all of us fiery Italians do," Tessa said, pausing to gather her thoughts. "Can we please put it behind us? It really has nothing to do with what's going on now. It was a long time ago." Tessa rose from the chair and abruptly left the room. I hoped she would accompany me this morning, because I was going out to search for Marco whether she came with me or not.

Gumdrop jumped into my lap. I pulled him close to me so we were face-to-face.

"Gummie, did you know Tessa had an Italian boyfriend before Craig?"

No response.

"Come on, Gumdrop. Tell me what you know."

"Yellooo?" His usual response. The cat jumped from my lap and headed for a warm spot on the Oriental rug by the window. "Thanks, Gummie, for being so helpful."

TEN

"JAX, OF ALL YOUR REALLY ROTTEN IDEAS, this may be your worst," Tessa said, as I pulled to the side of the road at the top of the slope by the river in Carthage. A loud crunch emanated from beneath the Ladybug as we came to a stop.

"I sure hope that wasn't anything serious," I said, getting out of the car and peeking under it. All I could see was mud. I flipped the back seat forward and Stanley the basset hound did his best to leap from the car. He needed a little help with his back end, so I gently lifted his hindquarters from the footwell behind the driver's seat. He galumphed away and landed right in a puddle. We were all going to need a bath when this was over. I caught up with him and clipped a long leash onto the dog's collar.

"Do you really think Stanley can help us find something other than dog treats down by the river?" Tessa asked.

"Stanley is a basset hound—a hound. He's supposed to be able to track things."

"I don't know about him. He's probably never tracked a thing in his life," Tessa said, looking doubtfully at Stanley as he waded out of the puddle he'd landed in.

"We'll never know if we don't give it a try. Come on, Stanley," I said, squishing through the mud and grass down the bank toward the river. Stanley, realizing we had a mission to accomplish, took off at a trot down the slope, sliding as he went and pulling me along behind him.

"Hold on. Whoa! Stop!" I yelled. The dog was well trained by his previous owner, or "his guardian," as she would have called herself. He stopped in his tracks but continued sliding down the muddy hill, stopping inches from the river's edge as I stumbled along to catch up with him. Tessa followed at a much slower rate, gingerly picking her way to the river's edge.

"What now?" Tessa asked, finally arriving at my side and looking down at the river.

"I'm not sure how I get him started. In the movies, they usually have something for the dog to smell to get a scent."

"You haven't thought this out at all, have you?" Tessa said, blowing her bangs off her forehead. She was still distressed from this morning's talk about Dario de Luca, though I couldn't understand why. She herself said it all happened a very long time ago. I hoped she might eventually fill me in.

"Let's give it a try," I said, unclipping the leash from the dog's collar. "Okay, Stanley! Go!"

The brown river churned past us, as he snuffled along the muddy bank, his nose to the ground. He stayed close to the water's edge, at times coming dangerously close to falling in. I hoped he wouldn't end up in the river because I was in no condition to jump in and rescue him, especially given how deep the water was and how quickly it was rushing by. We slogged through the cattails, heading farther and farther away from the studio.

"Are you really hoping we'll find Marco's body?" Tessa asked.

"Yes, a body or footprints or something."

"Footprints? There are footprints all over the place."

"Some sort of clue about what happened to Marco or Dez." I wished I could have stopped to enjoy this beautiful spot by the river. It was by far the part I liked best about Carthage: the river, the rolling hills, and the lush conifers growing near the river's edge. But while we were on this grim mission, I didn't have the time or energy to do anything other than focus on the muddy riverbank and scan for a dead man, or men.

The dog slowed down near a clump of reeds and branches, pacing back and forth in front of it and finally stopping. Stanley had found something. Or, he was simply having a good time, it was hard to tell.

"Ah-roo!" Stanley howled. We ran to him as fast as we could through the muck.

"Help me look under here," I yelled. When Tessa caught up, we started moving the debris. Together we flipped a large pile of branches into the water.

Marco's pale, muddy body was wedged in the reeds in the narrow inlet below us. His red shirt was pushed up around his neck, revealing a gaping dark red hole above his left nipple. His eyes wide, he stared blankly at the gray sky above us.

Tessa and I fell backward into the mud and sat there in stunned silence. The stench of Marco's decomposing body hit us next. If we hadn't already been sitting, I'm sure I would have fainted from the smell.

"*Dio mio!*" Tessa said, as we scrambled up the slippery embankment, sliding back a step for every two that we took. When we reached the Ladybug, we were covered in mud and wet to the bone. Tessa grabbed her cell phone and started dialing. "Yes, hello. I'm calling to report a dead body at the river's edge about a half-mile west of Carthage."

"Is the sheriff coming?" I asked, after she hung up.

"The dispatcher said he would call him on the radio."

"Let's go to the studio. We can get help there. Abby will know where the sheriff's office is or know how to get in touch with him, or someone, who can help us," I said.

"I'm going to stay here and wait for the sheriff. I don't want Marco to disappear again."

"Ah-roo! Ah-roo!" Stanley howled from the bottom of the slope.

"Ah, geez, Stanley. I'll rescue you, don't worry." I slogged down to the river's edge and grabbed at the basset hound. He was slick with mud and it wasn't easy to get a firm hold on him. I caught hold of his collar and pulled as hard as I could. I wasn't strong enough to move him. I wished I'd made it to the gym more often, but that would have required me to have a gym membership, and gym clothes, and time in my busy day to get there.

"What's happening? Everything okay?" Vance yelled as he slogged toward us, a tarp wrapped around him like a cape.

"We found Marco."

Vance spotted the body in the reeds.

"Oh. I see. Bad news. Really bad news. Did you call the sheriff?" Vance asked.

"We did. I'm sure someone will be here soon," I said.

"Ah-roo! Ah-roo!" Stanley added.

"You need some help?" Vance asked.

"I do. Can you help me get Stanley back up the hill?"

Vance approached the dog. "Shhh, now hold still. Everything's going to be okay," he whispered in Stanley's floppy ear once he reached us. Vance Dalton: Hound whisperer. He pulled off his makeshift cape, tied two corners together, and placed the dog in the sling he'd created. Grabbing the opposite side, he dragged the dog, chariot style, up the hill.

All of us were covered in mud from head to toe. In Stanley's case, that was from the tip of his nose to the tip of his tail. I grabbed an extra sweatshirt from the trunk, laid it on the backseat, and helped Stanley into the car. I pulled myself into the Ladybug.

"My car's going to need a thorough cleaning once this mess is over," I said.

"I'm sorry, Jax, but your dirty car is the least of our worries right now." Tessa stood next to the car, still determined to stay with Marco's body.

I started the car and put her in gear, but she wouldn't budge. Her wheels spun in place.

"Come on, you can do it!" I said, coaxing the car along with a little pat on the steering wheel. The car shuddered, and for a moment it looked like she was going to break free from the mud. I pressed the accelerator. The engine revved faster and faster, but the tires just spun in place.

"You're not helping! You're digging yourself in deeper!" Tessa yelled. Vance pushed the car from behind, but it was no use. The Ladybug was stuck.

I turned off the motor and tipped my head back onto the headrest.

"Ah, crap. What are we going to do?"

"You could call Zachary," Tessa said.

"Oh, no. He would not be pleased. He specifically told you I should not be out here looking for bodies."

I called Old Firehouse Studio, but got no answer.

I dialed Val's number next. "Can you get me out of a mess?"

"Oh, honey, that's my part-time job."

•   •   •

Fifteen minutes later, a black and gold sheriff's vehicle skidded to a stop next to us at the edge of the berm.

"I got a message forwarded from 911 dispatch. Did you find something?" Sheriff Poole asked, getting out of his car. Wordlessly, we all pointed down the slope toward the water's edge.

The sheriff looked down the slope at the corpse.

"Ah, hell, looks like a dead guy. Guess you girls were right," Sheriff Poole said. I sighed internally. Okay, maybe it was out loud.

He headed back to his cruiser and picked up his radio. An emergency vehicle arrived a little while later, and we watched while the sheriff consulted with the EMT and the ambulance driver about the best way to retrieve the body.

It seemed like it took forever for Val to arrive, but finally, Val's beat up Honda Civic came around the bend and zoomed toward us. At least I knew I'd soon be able to get out of these sopping wet clothes, and perhaps she could give the Ladybug a push with her car.

"Park here," I said, pointing to a wide spot of asphalt at the side of the road. We didn't want her car to end up like the Ladybug, axle-deep in mud.

"As requested, I brought you some clothes." She passed us a large pink tote through her car window. "T-shirts, pants, and some shoes. I grabbed some things from the guest room for you, Tessa." Val had a key to my side of the duplex. I often wondered how much time she spent over there when I wasn't home. So far, she hadn't tried to re-decorate while I was away, and for that, I was grateful.

"You are a life-saver," Tessa said, clutching the bag of clothes to her chest.

"Let's see what happened to the Ladybug. Maybe I can give her a push," Val said, getting out of her car. I glanced at Val's feet.

"What the heck are those?" I said gawking at her hard white plastic boots.

"Um. They're—" Val said.

"Wait a minute, I know what those are," Tessa said. "Joey loves Star Wars, but I won't let him watch most of it. It's too scary for a five-year-old."

"Are those stormtrooper boots?" I asked.

"Um, maybe?" Val said.

She looked ridiculous in her giant white plastic boots with her skin-tight leopard print leggings and an oversized puffy white parka.

"I'm giving them a test drive. I'm going to a science fiction convention with Rudy next week and I'm not sure if I can make them work, you know—"

"Can we talk about this later?" I asked Val. "We found a dead man." I pointed toward the river's edge.

"Oh my goodness! How horrible!" she said, fluttering a hand at her chest.

Sheriff Poole sauntered over to Val.

"Get a load of you. What's your name, honey?"

"Val," she replied. Under normal circumstances, Val would have flirted with this man. Instead, she reached out and put her hands on his shoulders. "You know, Sheriff, I'm happy to have met you." He gave her a lecherous grin. With a single movement, she flipped him around so he was pointed toward the river and gave him a shove.

"I think what you're looking for is down there," she said, as she pantomimed wiping her hands. I was certain this was a move Val had practiced, and used, on more than one occasion.

The sheriff sidestepped down the embankment, joining the EMT who had made his way down to the river's edge. The men unceremoniously dragged Marco up the embankment on a rescue board and onto a gurney at the back of the ambulance.

"Is this the EYE-talian who went missing?" the sheriff asked.

"It is. Where's he going?" I asked Sheriff Poole.

"King County Medical Examiner in Seattle," he said, looking down at the corpse. "Sure enough, here's a hole right in his chest. That's gotta be a stab wound." The sheriff looked like he was going to poke a stubby finger right into the hole. I interrupted him.

"Sheriff? I'm no expert, but you better not touch the body," I warned. Sheriff Poole pulled his finger away from Marco's chest.

"Oh, I wasn't going to touch him. Wouldn't want my DNA getting on the victim, right?"

"What's going to happen now?" I asked.

"First thing I've gotta do is fill out a bunch of paperwork. Probably have to get ahold of the EYE-talian embassy or something. Find the next of kin, all that stuff. Oh, and I guess I need to figure out who kilt this guy."

"I think it would be a good idea if you talked with a detective I know, but maybe you don't need to mention I was the one who found the body," I said.

"Now, see here. I've got this under control. You girls go back to playing with your little beads and glass geegaws. I've got to figure out what his family wants done with him. Do they want him back in Italy? You know, that sort of thing. I bet it'll cost a lot of money to ship a dead guy overseas."

"Probably can't use UPS," I said.

"You're right. Probably can't use FedEx either," the sheriff said.

ELEVEN

"**IF YOU WOULDN'T MIND**, can you give my car a push?" I asked the sheriff.

"I'll call a tow truck. I don't want to get my cruiser stuck in the mud along with you. Should only be a couple of hours before someone comes by for the car."

A couple of hours?

The sheriff's car peeled out, followed by the ambulance.

I wrote my phone number on a scrap of paper and left it on Ladybug's windshield along with a message that said I was at the glassblowing studio, so the tow truck driver could contact me when he arrived. There was simply no way I was going to sit around in the mud for hours waiting for someone to tow my car.

"I've got to get back to the salon," Val said. "I'll drop you off at the glass studio. Maybe you can get changed there and talk with the owner."

"What about Stanley?" I asked my neighbor. The dog was still sitting in the back seat of my car covered in mud and drooling.

"I'll take him with me and get him all cleaned up. He's probably too big to put into the shampoo bowl at the salon, but maybe I can get him into the shower at home," Val said, examining her long red nails and scraping out the mud from underneath them.

We transferred Stanley into Val's car, and Tessa climbed in back next to him. There wasn't room for anyone else back there, especially since half of one of the seats was piled with Val's shoes, which she often flung in the backseat when she wasn't wearing them. Stanley had picked up a red patent leather pump in his teeth and was chewing on it. Tessa grabbed it from him and gave him a stern look while wiping the slobber off the shoe's slightly gnawed-on heel.

"Looks like there's no room for me," Vance said. "That's okay, I'll walk back. It's not too far." Vance was possibly the kindest man I'd ever met. I hoped someday he'd meet the perfect woman. He'd recently divorced his wife, who had a penchant for bondage. While they had tried to patch things up, Vance had finally left after being spanked one too many times.

"Do you want me to come back and get you?" Val asked.

"No, I'm cool. I can take a shower in the studio once Tessa and Jax are done."

Val dropped us at Old Firehouse Studio and took off up Main Street. She rolled down the window in the back seat so Stanley could stick his head out. His enormous ears flopped gently in the wind as he held one of Val's shoes in his mouth.

"Let's find Abby and tell her the news, then we can find out what we're going to do now that class is over for good. Abby will have to face the fact that Marco is dead and not on some drunken road trip with Dez," Tessa said.

We found Abby in her office working on her computer. She seemed surprised to see us.

"What are you two doing here? You know class is postponed, right?"

"I'm sorry, Abby. We have some horrible news. We found Marco's body in the river. The sheriff is taking care of getting him to the morgue," I said.

"Marco's really dead?" Abby said, in barely a whisper. "I thought he'd be with Dez. If Marco is dead, what about Dez? Where is he? Maybe he's not on a bender after all." Abby drew a deep shuddering breath.

"Don't worry. I'm sure he's okay," Tessa said, grabbing hold of Abby and trying to hug her. Abby resisted, not wanting to be comforted.

"How could this have happened? A major glass artist comes to my studio and ends up dead...drowned in the river." Abby dropped into a chair and started to cry. Since Marco's official cause of death had not yet been determined, I decided to keep my mouth shut and not clarify that Marco had, in fact, died from a stab wound.

Duke sauntered into the cramped office and leaned against the doorjamb, arms crossed.

"So, class is canceled?" he asked.

"I just found out a second ago. Marco de Luca is dead. So, yes, class is canceled. I'll be making arrangements with you and the other students to make sure you are scheduled in to one of our other classes."

"What do you mean 'other classes'?" Duke asked, as surly as ever. "I paid for this class, and if I can't—"

"You can't have this class anymore, can you?" Abby snapped, coming unhinged. "Our damn teacher is dead. What do you expect me to do? Raise him from the dead, like you're trying to do with your glass career, you old has-been!" She leapt from her chair toward him. Tessa caught Abby by the arm before she attacked Duke physically.

"Listen, I can't help that you've gotten yourself in so deep with this studio that you're going to try and rip us off for our class fees. I want my money back. And I want it back now!" Duke was shouting at this point. He looked at us. We didn't make eye contact with him, not wanting him to pull us into his battle. I knew I wanted a refund. I'd never be a glassblower, but I also knew that right now was neither the time nor the place to make demands on an already frantic Abby.

"Don't worry about us. We can talk about our tuition later," Tessa said, reaching out to hug Abby again. Brittle with anger, Abby didn't return Tessa's hug. Duke and Abby stood there, silently seething, neither of them moving. Tessa and I slunk out of the office and went in search of the shower, which we found in the bathroom next to the kitchen.

"You go ahead and shower. I'll take one after you're finished. I need to call Zachary," I told Tessa. "If he hears from someone other than me that I found Marco's body, he's going to be pissed off. But if he finds out from me—"

"He'll be equally pissed off," Tessa said, heading toward the bathroom for a much-needed shower.

I stepped into the utility yard for some privacy and dialed Zachary's number.

"Grant," he said, in his usual serious tone.

"It's Jax. We found Marco."

"Drunk and alive?"

"I'm sad to say he's very, very dead."

"You didn't just stumble across him, did you? You went searching."

"I'm sorry, but yes, I did. The sheriff wasn't going to do anything. At least now he knows a crime's been committed and will take the case seriously, though it doesn't seem like he knows how to investigate, or—"

"I'll do what I can to get the victim transferred out to our M.E."

"The sheriff said Marco is already headed to the Seattle Medical Examiner's Office."

"Great. The M.E. should be able to determine the cause and time of death and from there we can see what else, if anything, needs to happen."

"We know the cause of death. He was stabbed in the chest, right through the heart. It was hard to tell much more than that. He'd been soaking in the river for a while. Do you think you can help on this? Maybe come and see the crime scene or the body?"

"I'd love to see your body," said Zachary. "But I'd need an invitation."

"Detective, you might want to rephrase that."

"Uh, yes, well, I didn't mean your body, I meant the body," he said, flustered. "The corpse," he added, in case it still wasn't clear.

Poor Zachary. For all of his seriousness, with all the gruesome stuff he dealt with every day, he simply couldn't get the hang of how to deal with women, or at least with me.

"The sheriff seems a little reluctant to let anyone else do anything on this case," I said.

"Do you mean he's reluctant to have *you* do anything on this case?" Tessa and I had been involved in a murder investigation at a bead shop last year. During that time, Zachary had been nothing short of cold to me, and it was only after the investigation was over that he had warmed up to me. I did help him solve the crime, so maybe it was gratitude, or maybe my natural charm had melted his cold heart. I'd never been very good at being charming, so I wasn't exactly sure. Maybe he was just getting used to me.

"It's possible, but in general, I think the sheriff doesn't like people giving him any sort of advice. Like this morning, he was stomping all over the crime scene—"

"Jax?" he cut me off. "Professionals don't like a particular kind of person giving them advice. Do you know who they can't stand getting advice from? Amateurs."

"Are you calling me an amateur?"

"Aren't you?"

"I don't have a degree or a certificate or whatever," I said. Now I was the flustered one.

"A badge. You don't have a badge."

"I think it's a little too late for me to become a cop. I'm not even sure I could pass the physical test. Don't you have to be able to run a mile and be able to do ten push-ups?"

"Tread lightly, please. I'll see if I can make some headway on my end. We don't want any maniacs out there in the boondocks murdering anyone else, including you."

"Got it. Thanks." I hung up the phone. Tessa found me in the yard.

"The shower's all yours. Was that Zachary? How'd it go?"

"Exactly what I thought would happen. Whenever I try to help—"

"Interfere—"

"Whose side are you on? Whenever I feel I can help in an investigation, Zachary always turns into a jerk."

"He is doing his job. Your job, on the other hand, is to make beads and design jewelry," Tessa said. "But your job right now is to go take a shower. All the mud is drying out. You're starting to look like a swamp monster."

"Thanks, Tessa. I appreciate it," I said, trying to rub a little of my grime onto her newly-clean arm.

"What are friends for?" Tessa said, pushing me down the hall toward the bathroom.

•   •   •

The tow truck driver arrived a few minutes after I finished my shower. I went out to the parking lot to meet him.

"Here's your car, ma'am," the driver said, pointing to the Ladybug, hiked up on his towing rig. "Sign right here, and you'll be all set."

"What do I owe you?" I asked.

"This one's on me. It didn't take much to get your car out. I'll tell you, though, you might have some damage on your front suspension. You must've hit a big rock or something when you parked at the side of the road. If you want, I can take it down to my garage and take a look."

"Is she safe to drive?"

"I think so, but I can check. It won't take any time at all."

The man handed me his card: *Tony Stein, Automotive Genius*. The guy had a sense of humor, at least. The address of his garage was on Main Street in Carthage. He must own the car repair shop where Tessa and I hid the night she saw Marco's body in the hot shop.

I watched as Tony towed the Ladybug down Main Street.

"She's going to be all right, you know," Tessa said, coming up beside me.

"I know. I'm not worried about my car, just about everything else. I can't believe Marco's been murdered and that someone would dump him in the river. I can't get the image out of my head of how he looked after soaking for so long."

"Come on. Let's walk down to the café and have some lunch. I bet you're hungry. You'll feel better if you eat," Tessa said. In typical

Italian fashion, she wanted to feed me and make me feel better. "And maybe we can have a cup of coffee."

When we walked into the Robin's Nest Café, once again Carl was standing at the podium by the front door, a menu in his hand, a smile on his face, and a red apron around his waist.

"You're back!" he said, flashing his gleaming smile. "Are you here for more muffins?"

"Today we'd like a sit-down lunch," Tessa said.

Carl guided us to a table and handed us menus. "We serve breakfast all day, so here's that menu, as well as the one for lunch."

Tessa's eyes glimmered as she reviewed the menu.

"Chocolate chip waffles!" Tessa said.

"Sounds delicious. Maybe some bacon on the side?"

"Shouldn't take any time at all. We're past our morning rush," Carl said.

"And coffee. Lots of coffee," I said. "Why don't you join us for a cup?"

"You know, I don't usually join guests at their tables, but I tell you, getting to sit down is one thing I don't get much of an opportunity to do. We're having a quiet time right now, so what the heck!" Carl said, grabbing a chair from another table and pulling it up before remembering he still needed to get the coffee and put in the order. "Be right back." He hustled off to grab three mugs and the coffee pot. Back at our table, he set down the cups, each filled to the brim, and finally settled into his chair.

"You're here for the glass class. How's it going so far?" Carl said, looking from one of us to the other, nodding and smiling.

"Not going well," I said, taking a sip of coffee, which was pretty good for diner coffee. "Our teacher passed away." I decided to leave out the part about how he had died and that I'd found the body.

"I'm sorry to hear about Dez," Carl said. The flat tone in his voice told me otherwise.

"No, it's Marco de Luca, not Dez. He was a visiting instructor from Italy."

"Oh, I... I... thought, well, that's awful," Carl said, looking out the window, lost in thought.

"But Dez is missing. I guess you haven't seen him, have you?"

"No," Carl said, finally snapping out of his daze. "Of course, the sheriff would have come and asked me about Dez if he was dead, I suppose."

"I'm sorry, I don't understand," Tessa said, trying, and failing, to make eye contact with Carl.

"Dez and I have some old wounds that'll probably never heal. You know, ladies, I'm going to leave you to enjoy yourselves," Carl said, abruptly rising from his chair. "I'll go check on your meals."

Vickie brought out our meals a few minutes later. Plates full of waffles, chocolate, and bacon were an excellent boost to our morale, as were a few cups of java. After our amazing meal, Vickie stopped by again to fill our cups.

"You gals stay as long as you want. When you're ready to go, tap the bell and I can ring you up," Vickie said.

"What now?" I asked Tessa. "Do you want to head back to my house?"

"Doesn't seem there's much else to do here. Do you think your car is ready by now?"

"Only one way to find out. We might as well walk down to the garage and see what the mechanic found. I hope whatever is wrong with my car doesn't cost a lot. With the price of the class and only a few bead sales this month, I'm feeling a little tight right now."

"Do you need a refund from Abby for the class?" Tessa asked.

"I'm doing okay." It was hard making a living as a glass artist, but since Aunt Rita had left me a substantial sum of money after she died, along with the house I resided in, I knew I had a financial buffer, even during the months when I didn't have a positive cash flow. I could imagine Abby and Dez's struggle to keep their new studio afloat given the expenses of building and running such a large facility. The electric bills to keep the furnace running, alone, would break the bank. Unless they were independently wealthy, there would be no way for them to have built a state-of-the-art studio without going into debt. That, combined with what must've been a large financial outlay to get Marco de Luca here from Italy, it would have stretched anyone's bank account to its limits, and might even be the cause of Dez's drinking problem.

Our moods had improved after the scrumptious meal, although I was certain that our cheerfulness would be short-lived, once we returned to the dismal situation at Abby and Dez's studio.

We rang the bell at the cash register so we could pay and waited for Vickie to appear. As we stood there, we noticed a portrait of a young girl, about ten years old, behind the counter, with dozens of get-well cards taped in a wreath around it.

Vickie swung out of the kitchen door and chugged up to us.

"What a beautiful girl," Tessa said, nodding toward the portrait.

"Is that your daughter?" I asked.

Vickie reached up and touched the edge of the frame, inhaling deeply as she did.

Carl ran from the kitchen and grabbed Vickie in a big hug. "It's okay, Vickie. I'm here now." Carl turned his wife toward the kitchen and guided her away from us.

Tessa and I looked at each other.

"What was that about?" I asked.

"Sounds like something happened to the girl. Maybe it's Vickie and Carl's daughter?"

"I wonder what happened to her." We were going to have to find out. That was second on my list. The first thing was finding out who killed Marco de Luca.

I dropped twenty dollars by the register and we headed out the door with more questions than we had when we entered. We crossed Main Street to Tony's garage and found him lying on his back with only his feet sticking out from under the front of my car.

"Excuse me, is that you, Tony?" I asked.

"Sure is," he said, rolling out from underneath the Ladybug. "I tightened things up on the underside of your car. Fortunately, there's no damage. I don't usually get to work on nice, new cars like this one. Usually it's beat-up old pickups and such. See all this junk?" Tony pointed out the back door of the garage at the spare parts in heavy-duty plastic bins. "I hold onto a lot of it in case I can reuse it. My customers like to save a little money when I can install a recycled part rather than buying a new one." Tony pulled himself up to standing.

"So, I can take her?" I asked. "What do I owe you?"

"Do you have any beads like the one you have on? I'd like one for my sister," Tony said. I was wearing a bead with an ocean motif that I'd started making recently.

"Sure. I can bring you one." Trading beads for a car repair? That was my kind of deal.

TWELVE

AFTER PICKING UP MY CAR from Tony, we headed back to my house, since it was clear nothing else was going to happen at the studio.

"Do you feel like a little treasure hunting?" Tessa asked as we entered my studio. She was looking at the attic stairs.

"Treasure hunting? Do you want to look in my attic? If you do, I think you may mean spider hunting," I said.

"When I was cleaning up our attic to get ready for the remodel, I found some amazing things, like an old tin cup from the 1920s and a calendar of pin-up girls from the 1940s. I don't know what I'll do with them, maybe sell them on eBay, but it's the hunt that's the most fun."

"I've only been in my attic once, for about thirty seconds, and it was scary. Sorry, not today."

"Aren't you curious? You don't care what amazing, maybe even valuable, things are up there?" Tessa asked, ready to dash up the staircase. I wasn't going to get her to settle down until I'd made at least a modest effort to explore what was lurking above our heads.

"Okay, okay. We'll take one brief look up there. We're going to spend five minutes. Got it? Five." Usually it was Tessa's role to be the bossy one, but right now, it was my turn. I'd been through too much to want to spend the rest of the day dodging cobwebs and sorting through bits and pieces of my great-aunt's belongings.

"Get a flashlight! We need some light," Tessa said. I grabbed the Maglite by the back door and headed for the stairs. Tessa was already halfway up the staircase and started passing down boxes of beads to me. Since I never used the steps, I'd turned it into one more place where I could store beads. I'd have to put them back when we were done so my studio wouldn't turn into an obstacle course of bead boxes. Tessa turned the attic doorknob and pushed open the door. The hinges screeched as the door swung open. Inside, it was as I remembered it: cobwebs hanging from the ceiling, a chair covered in a sheet—looking ghostly—and a few small boxes crammed into corners. One of the boxes contained the tiles that I'd found in my only other foray into the attic. Some of those tiles were now installed in my studio.

"Are you satisfied?" I asked, as I sat on the top stair next to her, peering in. "This was fun, let's do it again sometime." I stood up, ready to pull the door shut. Gumdrop cruised up the stairs to see what we were doing. He wasn't the most adventurous cat, but he did have a way of causing trouble. As I closed the door, Gumdrop jumped between Tessa and me and into the attic. I grabbed for him, but he slipped through my hands and scampered off into the darkness. His paws left a little trail of cat footprints in the dust on the attic's floorboards as he scurried away to the far side of the attic.

"Gumdrop! You come back this instant!" My cat did not understand English, but he did understand when someone was yelling at him. I adjusted my tone. "Gummie, here kitty-kitty-kitty." I swept the flashlight across the attic. His eyes flashed bright green as the light passed over them. He sat against the far wall, looking as gray as everything around him. All except for his vibrant eyes, which right now were staring at me mischievously. If I could have read his mind, he'd have been saying, "I bet you can't catch me."

I took a tentative step into the attic. Dust swirled around my ankles as I tiptoed toward my cat. As I passed the sheet-covered chair, I spotted a trunk I hadn't seen from the attic door.

"There's a trunk up here. I'm going to push it out the door. Be careful it doesn't squash you!" I hollered, as I shoved the wooden box out of the attic's opening.

As the trunk disappeared from view, there was a grunt on the other side of it. It had smashed Tessa a little more than I had intended. I reached Gumdrop and lunged toward him. He jumped through my outstretched arms and made a break for it.

"Gumdrop!" Tessa shouted as he ran over her lap and down the stairs. "Are you okay in there?"

"Yes. I'm on my way out. This is the last time I'm coming up here!" I turned slowly and headed toward the door, keeping my head low to avoid the spider webs, then inched my way back out. Tessa had dragged the trunk onto the top step so I could make my way out. I scrambled over the top of the trunk onto the steps below, a cloud of dust following me.

"Close the attic door before more dust escapes," I told Tessa. "Let's get this trunk downstairs."

With Tessa pushing, me pulling, and the trunk *thunk-thunk-thunking* down the stairs, we managed to get it to my studio floor. We sat next to the trunk admiring our newly-found treasure. I flipped the clips on its side and strained to push the lid open. The hinges, likely unopened for a decade or more, finally gave way. Inside were two colorful handmade quilts.

"They're beautiful. Do you think your great-aunt made them?" Tessa asked, running her hands over the fabric. She pulled out one of the quilts from the trunk and unfolded it. It had an intricate diamond pattern with tiny squares alternating in dark and light calico prints in pinks and greens. Safety pinned to the quilt was a note that simply said *For Connie*. While Tessa admired that quilt, I pulled the other one from the trunk. The design was similar to the first, but instead was made with tones of greens and blues. The note attached to it said *For Andy*. These were quilts my great-aunt had made for my brother and sister. I recalled Great-Aunt Rita's will listed two quilts that were for my brother and sister, in addition to my inheritance of the house. I'd never found the quilts and had wondered what had become of them. Had I realized they were in the attic, my siblings would have received their bequests three years ago. I'd make sure they got them now.

I found a small velvet sack under the quilts. While the quilts were in perfect condition, the bag at the bottom of the trunk looked older and much more fragile. I tugged open its drawstrings and gently pulled out the object within. It was a little ivory whale sculpture, no bigger than a deck of cards. It was amazingly intricate, and I wondered where it had come from and what its significance was.

"Do you think it's real ivory?" Tessa asked.

"I don't know, but it's got to be old. Maybe it's carved from a whale's tooth," I said, rubbing the side of the piece to see if there was an inscription. Gumdrop, who had been cleaning the dust off his long gray fur, sauntered over to see what we were up to.

Val burst in the front door.

"Hellooooo! Are you gals home?" Val called out from the foyer. "Come out, come out, where ever you are!"

"Let's keep this a secret for a while until we figure out what we've got here," I said. We hastily put everything back in the trunk, closed the lid, and pushed it under one of the worktables.

"We're back here in the studio," Tessa shouted to Val, then to me added, "we should act busy, so we don't look like we're hiding something."

I grabbed a metal cookie tin I'd been storing my most recent bead creations in and popped off the lid. Nestled in cotton balls inside was a necklace made with six round glass beads covered in tiny shell and coral designs. I'd strung them together with pink and white pearls and finished the piece with a seahorse-shaped clasp.

The trip-trapping of Val's high heels grew louder and louder as she walked through the house toward the studio.

"Jacqueline Renee O'Connell, you have outdone yourself!" Tessa exclaimed.

"Please don't call me by all my names, and especially not Jacqueline. You sound like my mother when she was angry with me."

"She did like to yell all of your names at you, didn't she?"

"Yes, she did," I said, picking up the necklace and running my fingers across the strands. "She still does."

"Hello, my little honeybunches! What are you doing back here?" said Val, flouncing through my studio door.

"Oh, us? Nothing," I lied.

"Nothing," Tessa repeated.

"Oh, good. I wouldn't want to hear that you two were digging up trouble!" Val said. She didn't know the half of it.

"What about you, has your mystery man come and gone? Are you back to normal now that you've finished making Tessa's delicious birthday cake?" I used the word normal in the broadest sense of the word. Val's version of normal was not that normal.

"Well, poo. I'm actually not normal at all. Rudy told me a couple of weeks ago we could go to the Burien UFO Festival. That's why I was trying out my stormtrooper boots. Now I'm furious because he says he's working on this big project, and, well, it sounds like there are delays, and it's going to back up his other projects and put him so far behind he's not going to get caught up for a while... Long story short, he said he can't take the time off."

"Delays?" Tessa asked. I knew what she was thinking. Rudy was working on her house this week as part of her big attic renovation. "Do you know what project?"

"Oh, some house in Ballard. Actually, now that you mention it, that must be your house."

"There cannot be delays. All of us are only gone for a week and then the house has to be ready to live in. My family of five cannot camp here with you until my house is finally done."

"Oh, sorry, Tessa, I don't know for sure if it's your house, maybe it's not your house."

"I'm calling the contractor!" Tessa said, stomping away to make the call in private.

"I'm sorry Rudy can't go to the festival. It happens with work. Sometimes you can't control your schedule."

"I took the time off from the salon, why couldn't he simply do the same?"

"Because he can't leave someone's house torn apart while he goes on vacation."

"I know, but still! You wouldn't want to go to festival with me, would you?"

"Sorry, I'm not a sci-fi girl."

"Oh, I know, I'm just disappointed. I was looking forward to going."

"I understand. We're disappointed with what happened with the class we're taking, only in our case, it's tragic. The class was canceled. The corpse you saw by the river? That was our teacher." While I was extremely distressed Marco de Luca was dead, I was not at all disappointed about the canceled class. I'd realized soon after we started that glassblowing was not for me.

"That was so awful! What were you doing down there?"

"We were searching—"

"For a specific dead guy, or trying to see what dead guys you could find in a river?" Val asked.

"We were looking for the instructor of our glassblowing class. He disappeared, and we thought we might find him in the river."

"Why did you think he'd be there?"

"I don't know. There was nothing else around. The river runs right behind the studio. It seemed to me if you were trying to hide a dead man, you'd take him down to the river and hope the current would carry him away."

"Good thinking, Jax! Way to think like a killer!" Val said. While this was supposed to be a compliment, it felt strange to be told I excelled at such evil thoughts.

"What's up with you? Why are you here?"

"Do you have any Tabasco sauce?"

"You're not going to try and make another one of your exploding spicy chocolate cakes again, are you?"

"No, my visitor would like some."

"Your visitor? Why are you being so secretive? Are you finally ready to tell me what's happening at your house?"

"No."

"No, what? No, you're not done being secretive, or no, you're not ready to tell me what's happening at your house?"

"Can you repeat the question?" Val asked, her red hair bouncing from side to side, as she shook her head.

"What's going on?"

"I, uh, well. I have a friend staying with me."

"Are you hiding someone over there?"

"I'm not exactly hiding him. That makes it sound like he's a fugitive."

"So, he's not a fugitive. That's a step in the right direction. Anything else you can tell me about him?"

"He's a man," Val said, sounding like she was giving up a huge piece of the secret.

"Yes, I figured that out because you are calling the person 'him,' using a male pronoun."

"Oh, poo. I guess I did give that one away."

"Anything else you're going to tell me?"

"He's a member of my family."

This took me totally by surprise. Of course, almost everyone had family members, even if it was only a mom or a dad. I'd never thought about Val's relatives other than the fact she felt like a member of my family, since I saw her so often.

"You didn't go out and get married or anything crazy like that, did you?" I asked. I doubted this was what she meant by a member of her family, but I never knew what Val would do, so a quick elopement wasn't out of the realm of reality for her.

"Of course not! I've said enough. I should go," Val said, trotting toward the door as quickly as she could in four-inch stilettos. She made a quick detour to grab the Tabasco from my fridge.

I found Tessa sitting at the bistro table on my back patio, talking on the phone. She finished and filled me in.

"My contractor was not available. I left him a message. I hope I wasn't too intense." She probably was. She can come across as pushy whenever she's stressed. "Then I called my mother-in-law's house and talked with Joey."

"That must've have cheered you up. Did it?"

"Oh, a little. Joey seemed glad to talk with me, but you know, he's not really the chatty type. Then I called Abby to see how things were going for her. She can't seem to figure out whom to call to inform about Marco's death. His phone is locked and she doesn't know the password on his computer, so she can't get to his contacts."

"What about Violetta?" I asked.

"Violetta was going to send some emails, but I haven't heard back from her. I've texted her, but she's not answered my messages," Tessa said.

"Wasn't Sheriff Poole going to talk to the Italian embassy? Maybe they can find his family?"

"Maybe, but, I…"

"What's up?" I asked. She sniffled a little. "Do you want to tell me about it?"

"I know how to find Marco's brother."

THIRTEEN

TESSA MADE SOME CALLS and finally tracked down her Uncle Guido. Through a mixture of English and Italian I understood that Marco's brother, Dario de Luca, was somewhere in California. She hung up the phone, an exasperated frown on her face.

"We've got to go see my Uncle Guido."

"But you talked with him a second ago."

"He says I owe him a visit. He's going to give me the scoop on Dario and tell me how to find him."

"Where's your uncle?" I asked.

"San Francisco."

"We're going to San Francisco?"

"Yes, we are," Tessa said. "We've got to do this. Dario needs to know his brother has passed away." Tessa paused and crossed herself as she often did when speaking of the deceased. "I want to be the one to tell him, and I want to tell him in person. He'll need to make arrangements for his brother's burial and tell his family."

"Tell me why we need to see your uncle? You're sure you can't call Dario?"

"Uncle Guido is sort of old-school. He does me a favor, I do him a favor."

"What favor are you doing for him?"

"He wants to see me. That's the favor. He says he never gets to see his favorite niece, and if I want to know how to find Dario, I'm going to have to come down and see him in person."

"It's far too late to get a flight to San Francisco today," I said. Tessa had an intense look in her eyes. I'd seen it before a million times. She wasn't taking no for an answer. Defeated, I grabbed my laptop from my room and checked the flights on Alaska Airlines. Tessa saw the flight she wanted and pecked at the screen with her index finger.

"That's the one, right there."

"Tessa, that flight leaves in two hours."

"Perfect. We have enough to time to drive to the airport, park, and run to the gate. We can do this. We've got to do this."

"We could wait until morning," I said, hoping I could talk some sense into her. Tessa grabbed her handbag and my keys and headed for the back door. "No luggage?" I asked.

"No time."

• • •

Tessa climbed in the driver's seat of my car.

"This is my car, shouldn't I be driving?" I asked, as I reluctantly climbed into the passenger seat.

"Pshh, you're always so protective of the Ladybug." That was true. Tessa drove like a maniac, and I didn't want my car to get banged up. "We're heading straight to the airport. We can make the next flight to San Francisco if we hurry."

"We're seriously going to California? Aren't I usually the one with the outrageous plans?"

Without a word, Tessa jammed her foot down on the Ladybug's accelerator. Off we went, speeding toward the Seattle-Tacoma International Airport. As we drove down my street, a patrol car turned the corner and followed us.

"*Che casino*, there's a cop behind me!"

"You weren't speeding, were you?"

"No, I—" Flashing lights spun across the dashboard. Tessa found a gap between parked cars and pulled over slowly and carefully.

For the second time this week, we'd been pulled over. I prayed it was not Ryan. But, sure enough, it was.

"Do you know how—" Ryan said, tipping his head to look in the driver's side window.

"Do I know how fast I was going? No, but I'd say it was only a couple of miles above the speed limit," Tessa said.

"Tessa? I thought it would be Jax driving," Ryan said. "And, no—that's not the question. Do you know how long I've been waiting for you?"

"I don't know! How long have you been waiting to catch me speeding *again*—" Tessa replied, assuming Ryan was still talking with her. "Oh, wait, you mean Jax."

"I think it's really creepy that you're lurking around waiting for me," I said.

"I wanted to apologize."

"Apology accepted. Now, may we please go? We have a plane to catch."

"I'll call you!" Ryan said, as Tessa pulled away from the curb. It was strange that Ryan had gone from ignoring me to stalking me. I didn't like either of those behaviors. When I met him in Portland, he was nice, sexy, and very interested in me, but he seemed like an entirely different person now that he was in Seattle. I needed to ask Val for some lessons on how to deal with Ryan. However, I'd have to be patient and wait until she stopped hiding out with her mystery man next door.

"Are you sure you don't want me to drive?" I asked, clutching the door handle, as she took the freeway on-ramp at a roller coaster's pace. I held on for dear life as we zipped down I-5 to the airport.

"No, I've got this," Tessa said, gripping the steering wheel with a look of intensity on her face.

"This airline ticket is going to cost us a million dollars," I said.

"Don't worry, Uncle Guido said he'd take care of it. We've got to do this. It's the right thing to do." I was certain Tessa was excited, or nervous, to see Dario after all these years, but she'd never admit it. Tessa was convinced the most important thing she could do was to tell Dario about his brother, and once Tessa had something set in her mind, there was no stopping her.

• • •

We bought our tickets, miraculously breezed through security, and sprinted to the gate for final boarding. The plane was so full that Tessa and I had to sit rows apart. Fortunately, the flight was short, and we soon found ourselves at the rental car counter in the San Francisco International Airport.

"We've got you in a Ford Escort," said the clerk who was helping us, his black and yellow vest matching the Hertz sign above his head. "But for an extra fifty dollars we can put you into something sporty." Tessa was resigned to a boring compact car, but perked up as soon as the agent said 'sporty.'

"We'll take it," she said.

"Don't you want to know what it is?" I asked Tessa.

"No, I—"

"It's a Fiat," the clerk replied, as he continued typing on his computer keyboard.

"My dream car! I've always wanted a Fiat, but in Venice, there are only canals, no roads. No roads, no cars. And once I got back to the United States, I needed a family car."

"All right, here's the contract. Whoever is driving, please sign where it's highlighted," the clerk said. I reached for the clipboard, but Tessa snatched it away.

"I am driving for this trip. I am," Tessa said.

"No arguments from me."

Soon we were on the road. After a short trip on the freeway, we began winding our way through the streets of San Francisco. The first stop on our adventure was Uncle Guido's restaurant in North Beach, the Little Italy of San Francisco, where each lamppost had been painted with stripes in the colors of the Italian flag: red, white, and green.

Looking for a place to park the car, Tessa circled the blocks near the restaurant a dozen times, passing the Condor strip club, Italian delis, quaint outdoor cafés, and the City Lights Bookstore. I caught a glimpse of the verdigris-colored Zoetrope building and the Transamerica Pyramid as Tessa zoomed up and down the hilly streets, grinning like a fool. We finally found a parking spot and wedged the Fiat into a space between two driveways. We walked down a steep street to the restaurant, pushed through the door, and found ourselves face-to-face with Uncle Guido himself.

"*Zio Guido!*" Tessa said, hugging him and kissing him on each cheek.

"It has been too long since I've seen your pretty face," Uncle Guido said, pulling Tessa into view. "And this? Who's this?"

"This is my best friend in the whole world, Jax O'Connell."

I extended my hand to shake, and instead he grabbed me by the shoulders and kissed my right cheek, then my left. "Any friend of Tessa's is a friend of mine."

"We're famished!" Tessa said. "It's been a long day. Is it possible to get dinner?"

"Of course, of course! Come right this way. I've got a lovely booth here by the window." We slid onto the enormous red vinyl seats, facing each other.

"You still like *polpette*? I've got some fresh," asked Guido.

"*Si, prego*. I'd love some," Tessa said.

"And you, miss, what would you like?"

"Geez, ah, I haven't had time to look at the menu. I guess I'll have what she's having," I said.

"Two orders of polpette, coming up," Guido said.

"Are you going to tell me what the situation with Dario is?" I asked Tessa. "When you said things didn't end well, what did that mean?"

"My family wanted me to marry someone in the glass world. You know, my grandparents, they were prominent in Venice. They wanted to make sure I married someone who also had a strong Italian connection to glass, and that was the de Luca family. My grandparents had hoped that the two families coming together would ensure the future of them both and the future of Venetian glass."

"It seems like a lot to place on your shoulders."

"It was. I broke my grandparents' hearts when I married Craig and moved away. They wanted me to stay in Venice, to marry a nice Italian man, and raise my children there."

"And that was Dario? He certainly can't be upset with you after all this time. Why don't you give him a call?"

"He's the kind of guy who would take off before we got there so he wouldn't have to confront me."

Uncle Guido arrived with a basket of hot garlic bread and a big white bowl, which he placed in front of Tessa. It was pasta topped with what looked like tiny tentacles.

"Enjoy! I'll go get Jax's plate," Guido said with a little bow.

"What are those?" I asked Tessa.

"Polpette—little baby octopi on a bed of linguine. I was surprised you ordered them too."

"I didn't know that's what they were! I thought *polpette* were meatballs," I said, my voice raising a few octaves.

"Oh, I'm sorry, Jax…"

Guido bustled toward us with another white dish. I closed my eyes when my meal arrived, scared to look inside the bowl. When I finally peeked, I was amazed to see meatballs and pasta.

"I thought you'd prefer this kind of polpette," Guido said, with a wink.

"Thank you very much, Guido," I said, relieved he'd sized me up as the kind of person who wouldn't want miniature cephalopods for dinner. After eating the entire bowl of pasta, some crispy garlic bread, and a piece of tiramisu to die for, I couldn't eat another bite.

Uncle Guido joined us at the table, bringing a cappuccino for each of us. He sat down next to Tessa, pushing the cup in front of her.

"And my dear niece, how are you? How are your children? How is that American husband of yours?" While Uncle Guido peppered Tessa with questions, I drank my coffee and then stepped outside to call my brother.

FOURTEEN

"HEY, BIG SIS!" Andy said, answering his phone. "What's up?"

"I'm in San Francisco with Tessa. We're on a mission to find a friend."

"Any friend, or someone in particular?"

"Very funny."

Tessa joined me at the curb, smiled, and flashed a business card with a note written on the back.

"We're trying to find a man who Tessa knew many years ago in Venice," I told my brother. "We're headed to…where are we going, Tessa?"

"Napa," she replied, reading the note on the card she received from Uncle Guido.

"Not a good idea," Andy said, hearing Tessa's answer. "Do you have any idea what the traffic will be like this time of night going over the Golden Gate Bridge, through Marin County, and up to Napa? It'll take you hours."

"Hours?" If we were going to find Dario, looking for him late at night didn't seem like the best idea.

"Come stay with me. I have a terrific new apartment, and I actually have some free time." Andy's start-up software company, Pook, had kept him working all day, every day for the past year. All his hard work had paid off, so he was doing well financially, certainly better than I was. "We released a new version of our software last week and I don't have much to do right now until we start working on the next set of features."

"Hold on, let me check with Tessa," I said, covering my phone. "He's invited us to stay with him for the night. What do you think? Can we wait until morning to find Dario?"

"It is getting pretty late, and besides, who wants to sit in traffic when we could be speeding along in our little Fiat in the morning? Fiats are meant to be driven fast."

"We'll take you up on your offer," I said. Andy gave us directions to his apartment, which was located in a neighborhood called Dog Patch. The area was much nicer than the name implied. Andy lived in a brick building that had clearly once been a warehouse, but had been renovated into elegant, modern apartments. He buzzed us in when we arrived, and we took the stairs up to the second level. He was waiting for us in his doorway with arms open wide.

"Great to see you," Andy said, giving me a big hug.

"Andy! *Dio mio!*" Tessa said, grabbing him by the shoulders and pulling him into a hug. "I haven't seen you since you were a kid. Look at you, all grown up."

"And these are pretty impressive digs you have here. Your company must be doing really well," I said.

"Yeah, all my stock options helped me get this apartment. Rents are astronomical in San Francisco," Andy said, ushering us in. "Where are your bags?"

"It was a spontaneous trip. No overnight bags for us," I said.

"I'll get you some clothes that you can wear as pajamas." Andy headed to his bedroom. Tessa and I took a seat on his black leather sofa, a shiny chrome and glass coffee table in front of us. While it wasn't a large apartment, it was stylish—all black and silver—but a little sterile. In the corner of the living room, a TV-sized computer monitor sat on a large sleek desk. I was certain this was where Andy did most of his coding when he wasn't at the office. The screen saver, a swirling rainbow of colors spinning across the monitor, was the only artistic thing in the room. He had no art on the walls, and his shelves held only computer programming books.

Andy came back a few minutes later with a pile of clothes.

"Here you go. Pick out what you want, and we can wash what you're wearing," Andy said.

In the bathroom, predictably in white and silver with white towels, Tessa and I changed into the sweats and T-shirts Andy had given us.

"Sorry for the delay in getting to Dario," I said, pulling on a shirt that said *It's not a bug, it's an undocumented feature*. I had no idea what that meant, but the fabric was soft, and it would work well as a nightshirt.

"It's okay, I think it's best we find him in the morning. I'm not sure what we'd find up there at night. I'm not even sure what we'll find during the day."

Andy was sitting in front of his computer monitor when we returned to the living room.

"Don't tell me you're working," I said.

"No, I was doing a favor for a friend." He'd done a favor for me last year when I needed a background check on a man I was dating, so I knew what kind of semi-legal research he could do for friends and sisters.

"Do you think you could find something out for me about a family I know in Carthage, Washington?" I asked my brother. They have a daughter who may have died or is very ill." I hadn't been able to shake Carl's strange reaction when he thought Dez had died, and how Vickie and Carl had been so overwhelmed with sadness when I asked about their daughter.

"Sure, but we don't need my digital breaking and entering skills to do that," Andy said. "What's the name of the girl or the family's last name?"

"We don't know," Tessa said, pulling up a chair next to the desk.

"How about the first names of the parents?" Andy asked.

"Carl and Vickie," I said.

"You're not giving me much to go on. Let's see Carl and Vickie, Carthage, Washington..." Andy said, typing.

A few minutes later, we had our answer.

"Robin Nest. That's the girl," Andy said.

"It's got to be her. Her parents own a café called Robin's Nest, so it fits," I said.

"It says here she was critically injured last summer in a hit-and-run accident on Main Street in Carthage."

"Oh, no, that's awful! No wonder Carl and Vickie have their daughter's portrait framed with get well cards at the register in the café. Does it say if they found the person who hit her?" Tessa asked.

"No, but if you want me to find out, I need to use my not-very-legal skills. So, you both better go to bed. It's best if no one see this next part. No witnesses, no crime."

"I'm pretty sure that's not true," I said. Andy sounded like Sheriff Poole—no dead body, no crime.

"I changed the sheets on my bed so you can sleep in my bedroom and I'll sleep on the sofa," Andy said.

"Oh, hey, that reminds me. I was up in the attic in my house and I found a patchwork quilt that Great-Aunt Rita made for you. Do you want it?"

"Uh, Jax? I don't think it would fit my décor, do you?"

"Well, no, but it's a family heirloom..."

"I'm sure you can find a better use for it than sending it down here. I certainly won't ever use it."

"Suit yourself," I said.

"Sorry you have to share a bed," Andy said as Tessa and I headed for the bedroom.

"I don't mind sharing with Tessa, as long as she doesn't snore," I said.

"Of course I don't snore! I hope you don't snore," Tessa muttered.

FIFTEEN

I WOKE UP the next morning to the smell of coffee That was always a wonderful way to start the day. I padded out to the kitchen and grabbed a cup. Andy was still sitting at his computer where we'd left him.

"I hope you haven't been up all night working on this favor for me," I said, pouring myself a cup of coffee. "More coffee?"

"No, I'm good."

"What did you find out?" I said, taking my first glorious sip of java. "Ahh."

"I think you have a serious coffee addiction. You'd fit right in with everyone here in The City."

"*The City*? What does that mean? Seattle is a city, but we don't call it The City when we're talking about it."

"It's just a San Francisco thing," Andy said, shrugging. "So, here's what I've got. It looks like the girl, Robin, was seriously injured, crushed by the car that hit her. There was a lawsuit, Carl and Vickie Nest versus some people named Abigail and Desmond McCabe."

"Abby and Dez. The Nests think Dez ran over their daughter?"

"That's what the court records say. It says here the case was thrown out due to insufficient evidence."

"What's up?" Tessa asked, joining us at the computer.

I explained to Tessa what we'd learned about the hit-and-run accident.

"Given what Dez is like today, drinking and driving all over the place, it wouldn't surprise me if he did hit the poor girl," Tessa said.

"It sure would explain why Carl hates Dez so much," I said. "It also means that if Dez is missing, it might be because Carl, or Vickie, for that matter, had something to do with it."

"That's a pretty big leap to make. We don't even know if Dez is dead. But it's a huge coincidence that something terrible would happen to both Marco and Dez on the same night," Tessa said.

"One thing we do know: Marco is dead. We should get on the road and find Dario so we can tell him the news," I said.

• • •

Back in our little black Fiat, we headed north toward Napa.

"Why didn't you ever tell me about Dario?" I asked. In the time right after we had graduated from high school, when Tessa had moved to Italy and I'd gone to the University of Miami to get a degree in biology, we'd lost touch for a few years. It must have been during the time when we drifted apart that she dated Dario de Luca. She'd never mentioned him to me before, so perhaps he hadn't been important to her.

"Oh, you know, he was a chapter in my life. Why bring it up when it's ancient history?"

"I feel like I missed out on a big part of your life."

"I was in my early twenties and was living in Venice. It was such a beautiful, romantic place. I mean, how could I help myself? My grandparents wanted to find me a man. To be honest, I was excited when Dario, from the famous de Luca glass family, wanted to go out with me."

"But what did you want?"

"I wanted to have fun. I was young, he was cute and liked to spend money on fancy dinners and outings. Venice is possibly the most romantic city in the world. But after a while, I realized there was more to life than romance—I needed real love to make my life complete. When I met Craig, he was an intern at the American Embassy and didn't have a cent. He was living in the youth hostel in Guidecca, on the far side of the Grand Canal. I'd go and visit him whenever I could, even when it meant I had to take a boat all the way around the island to get there. I loved his laugh, and he could make me smile by doing the smallest things. We connected in so many ways. I knew he was the one."

"And Dario, how did he take the news?"

"I didn't get a chance to tell him myself. I told my nonna I was in love with Craig, and she flew off the handle and stormed over to the de Luca's palazzo to tell them the news. I left for Seattle soon after, and never had the opportunity to talk with him."

"Things must have been rough with your family after that."

"They were at first, but they got over it when I had Izzy."

"I've always wondered, were your parents disappointed you didn't give your kids Italian names?"

"But I did. Izzy is Isabella, Ashley is Alessandra, and Joey is Giuseppe."

"Joey's real name is Giuseppe?"

"It's on his birth certificate. My parents made me promise I would give him a proper Italian name."

"Will your kids spend time in Venice like you did?"

"Only if they want to. I'm not going to force them. They're part of a new generation. They don't even speak Italian. Maybe someday they'll want to embrace their Italian heritage, but we'll cross that bridge—"

"Speaking of crossing bridges, look at the gorgeous view of the Pacific Ocean," I said. With the windows down, we glided over the Golden Gate Bridge, high above the mouth of the glittering San Francisco Bay.

●　　●　　●

Guido told us we needed to head to Napa Valley, home, some would say, of the best wine-making grapes in the world. Tessa told me Dario owned a winery, gallery, and restaurant called *Vino e Vetro*, which meant "wine and glass." It sounded much better in Italian than in English.

After a two-hour drive, we found the place. It lived up to its elegant name. Arched metal gates stood open at the entrance to a winding, crushed granite driveway lined with olive trees. As we rounded a bend, *Vino e Vetro* came into view: A perfect Tuscan villa with acres of grapevines surrounding it. Tessa parked, and we crossed a terra-cotta tiled patio to an open pair of carved wooden doors.

"Hello?" I called, peeking in the doorway. There was no response.

"*Buongiorno*," Tessa tried in Italian. It didn't seem like it would help, given that no one answered me in English. But, I was wrong.

"*Buongiorno*," replied a man's voice from behind us.

We turned as the man approached from the far end of the patio. He saw Tessa and he stopped in his tracks. I saw the similarity to his brother, although Dario de Luca was more slender and not as muscular as Marco had been.

"Tessa? How can you be here? Why are you here?" Dario asked, staring intently at my friend.

"Dario, I have some sad news for you. I wanted you to hear from someone you know," Tessa said.

"I can't believe you're here. Tell me, what is wrong?"

"My friend Jax and I," she said, gesturing toward me, "were taking a class with your brother. He, well…it breaks my heart to tell you this. Marco is dead."

"What? No, that can't be," Dario said, shaking his head, refusing to hear what Tessa said.

"I'm sorry, Dario, but it's true," she said.

"Very sorry," I echoed, my hand on Tessa's shoulder.

"But, I don't understand. He was in Seattle. He emailed me. He said he was going to come down after his class. And what are you doing down here? I thought you lived in Seattle."

"I do live in Seattle, we both do," Tessa said, patting my hand. "Something happened at the glassblowing studio. I'm so very sorry your brother is gone." When Tessa said, "something happened," this was her way of skipping the part about finding his brother at the edge of a river with a stab wound through his heart.

Dario sank onto a bench at the edge of the patio and looked up at Tessa. There was despair in his eyes, but they were dry. Tessa's and mine, however, were getting pretty teary.

"But, how? What happened?"

"I'm sorry, this will be hard for you to hear. Marco was murdered."

"No. It can't be..." Dario closed his eyes tightly and turned his head, not wanting us to see him cry.

"I'm sorry that after all these years, this is how we see each other again," Tessa said, sitting down next to Dario.

"I am, as well," said Dario. "You know, I'm not angry anymore about how things ended. Neither of us wanted what our grandparents did."

"I'm glad you understand. I've always cared about you and didn't want you to find out about Marco from a stranger."

"My deepest sympathy," I said, feeling awkward that I was intruding on an intimate conversation between old friends.

"Why didn't you call before coming today?" Dario asked.

"Because I was afraid you wouldn't want to see me."

"Of course I would want to see you," said Dario.

"We need to put you in touch with the authorities so you can tell them what you'd like to do with Marco's body. Maybe you'll want to send him back to your family in Italy?"

"No, we need to bury him here. He belongs with me. There is no one else. Mama passed away last year, and Papa two years before her. I was all Marco had, and he was all I had. Our parents left us an inheritance. That's why Marco was coming to see me. Now that the estate is settled, I was going to complete the process of dividing the assets."

"I'm so sorry," Tessa said, clasping one of Dario's hands.

"Who was it? I must know. Who killed my brother?"

"We don't know. The police are searching for the culprit," I said.

"We must find him, whoever it is. He must be brought to justice!"

"Tessa and I are going to help find the killer, we promise," I said. Almost any other time, Tessa would have corrected me in a variety of ways, including that we were not going to try to find the killer and that she was not going to assist me.

"I must help as well. Please. For my brother. What can I do?"

"You don't have to do anything," Tessa said. "You need to take care of yourself and make arrangements for your brother."

"No. I am coming with you. This is important for me. I will make arrangements for Marco in Seattle. There is nothing I can do here by myself."

"Is it okay with you if Dario stays at your house?" Tessa asked me. "I don't want him to be all alone in a hotel room,"

"No, I don't want to impose," Dario added.

"Of course. We'll make room," I said firmly, wishing I'd already converted my attic into a guest room.

"I can help with the investigation," Dario said.

"We have to be careful about snooping around," Tessa said. "We don't want to raise anyone's suspicions, so we'll have to keep this quiet. We don't want anyone to get angry about what we're up to, like the sheriff—"

"Or Zachary," I added.

"Or the killer for that matter," Tessa said. "I know what we'll do. You can teach the class."

"It's the perfect ruse," I agreed. "Dario, if you teach the class, maybe you can help draw out the killer. Marco was killed at the studio, so the killer is most likely someone at Old Firehouse Studio or from Carthage."

"Oh, no, I don't work with glass anymore. Marco, he was the famous one. Me? I'm better with grapes, wine, and Italian food. I love glass, but don't make it anymore. I only sell it in my glass gallery. We have some lovely pieces made by other artists."

"But just because he had the fame doesn't mean he was any better than you. You were always the artist. Marco was more of a showman," Tessa said.

"*Amica mia*, Tessa. You are so honest. Such a good woman. Craig is a lucky, lucky man to have you. I will teach the class, and we will find the person who killed my brother. Now, you both must be hungry after your long journey," said Dario, who, like Tessa, seemed to think, and rightly so, that food can soothe troubled souls. He led the way toward the restaurant on the far side of the vineyard.

The tables in his restaurant were located beneath an arbor covered with grapevines, their newly-opened leaves pale green in the sunlight. Dario spoke in Italian to the server. I didn't understand a single thing he said to her, but I was certain that whatever it was he'd ordered for us would be delicious.

"Food is love, and we could all use a little of both right now," Dario said, pouring us each a glass of wine as the server brought over bread, cheese, and olives. "And while we are sorrowful, we will toast to the good life my brother had. I loved my brother—"

"To Marco de Luca," Tessa said.

"To Marco," I added, raising my glass.

Dario, saying nothing more, afraid his voice might give way to tears, simply touched his glass to ours, and drank.

Our lunch was exquisite; each course was a delightful surprise: butternut squash soup, crispy flatbread with rosemary, a light salad of mixed greens, and a perfect crème brûlée. Tessa stopped drinking after her first glass, since she knew she'd be driving us back to the airport. Thanks to an attentive server who refilled my wine glass each time it was empty, I was a little tipsy by the end our meal. I kept my eye on Dario, wondering how he was doing, having received such shocking news. Feeding us seemed to help his spirits, but I could tell he was in tremendous pain under his suave exterior.

•   •   •

"Okay, we've got three hours to make it back to the airport for the last plane to Seattle," Tessa said to Dario, who was in the passenger's seat next to her. "Are you okay back there?"

"Sure, I'm fine," I said. It was cramped in the back seat of the Fiat, which was more of a two-person car. It wasn't that there was a small amount of backseat legroom; there was no legroom at all. As Tessa drove, I kept my knees pulled up toward my chest, alternating with stretching my legs across the seat until they started to cramp. Neither of these positions were comfortable for a middle-aged—pre-middle-aged, that is—woman for longer than a few minutes

We arrived home late that night after a long journey to the San Francisco International Airport, a cramped Alaska Airlines flight to Seattle, and a thirty-minute drive to my house. It felt like an eternity since we'd left to find Dario. I was exhausted. I didn't have a place for him to sleep, and that was going to be a bit of a problem. If I sent him over to Val's, we might never get him away from her, although it sounded like her mystery guest might be keeping her busy. Tonight, I wished I had a cute little guest room in my attic. Dario was far too tall to fit onto my velvet sofa in the living room, which meant I'd be sleeping there, while I gave up my own bed to him.

I pulled out some extra blankets from the linen closet, and headed toward the sofa.

"Are you sure you don't want me to take the sofa?" Tessa asked when she met me in the hall.

"No, it's okay. It won't be for long. You're all settled in the Bead Lair, so you should stay. There's no sense in you moving," I said.

"I am sorry to be taking your room. Thank you for your kind hospitality," Dario said.

"Listen, both of you, I'm fine. It's really no big deal," I said. After all, he had lost his brother. He needed all the comfort he could get, and that meant a room of his own—my room, and my cozy bed.

SIXTEEN

THE NEXT MORNING I woke up and rolled over, nearly falling off the sofa. Dario was moving silently around the kitchen making coffee and scrambling eggs. Two pieces of toast popped out of the toaster.

He glanced over and saw me looking at him.

"Good morning, Jax. Are you ready for some coffee?" he asked. He waited for my nod and handed me a cup.

"Thanks," I said. What a gem. Tessa made an interesting choice by marrying Craig instead of this sexy Italian man. Craig was a terrific guy, but more cuddly than sexy. My friend followed her heart, and I understood that, even if her parents and grandparents hadn't.

Gumdrop was purring and rubbing up against Dario's legs while he moved around the kitchen. Usually Gummie didn't like the men I brought home, although he had warmed up to Zachary when he came over on Valentine's Day a few weeks ago.

Tessa shuffled out a little later.

"And for you, dear Tessa," Dario said, handing her a cup of coffee with a flourish and a smile. She smiled, gave him a hug, and curled up in the paisley chair.

I called Abby.

"You are not going to believe who is standing here next to me,"
I said.

"I hope it's Dez, because he's still missing, and if I don't find him
soon, I'm going to lose my mind."

"Dario de Luca."

"You've gotta be kidding me."

"Tessa and I went to San Francisco to tell him the news about his
brother. We convinced him to come back with us. And guess what?
He said he can step in and teach the class, now that Marco is, you
know...no longer able to."

Tessa grabbed the phone from me.

"Listen, Abby, I've known Dario for a very long time. He is at
least as good as Marco ever was at creating murrine. He's here, and
he's going to teach the class. Okay?"

I grabbed the phone back.

"You find the students, and we'll bring the teacher."

"I guess we'll have to see if anyone complains. Better than canceling
class, that's for sure. Good work, both of you. I owe you one, hell, I
owe you ten! I'll call the students and tell them we'll start back up
today."

"Great! We'll be out there with Dario in another hour or so."

While Dario was a terrific guy when making breakfast, he
turned out to be a wreck when it came to getting ready to leave.
Tessa was waiting impatiently with me as I sat on the sofa in my
pajamas, nursing an almost cold cup of coffee, while he used my
bedroom to get ready.

"I can't even get to my clothes. They're all trapped in my room
with Dario," I told Tessa. We sat for a few more minutes, and then
I'd had enough.

"Are you about finished in there?" I asked, knocking on the bedroom door. "I need to get ready to go."

"I need one more moment," he said.

I stomped back out to the living room. "He needs one more
moment. I'm hoping his moments and minutes are the same thing."

When Dario finally appeared, he looked fine. Why it had taken him thirty minutes to look that way, I had no idea. It took me five minutes to get dressed and I was back on the sofa with Tessa. After waiting for him again while he finished getting ready in the bathroom, we finally left. It was a good thing Tessa was so petite. She fit in the Ladybug's cramped back seat with no problem. The rain was coming down steadily again, and the car's wipers sloshed the water off the windshield at the fastest speed possible as I drove toward Carthage. When we arrived at the studio, we ran through the parking lot in the rain to the warm studio. I hoped when we got inside we'd find a group of students and not just an empty hot shop.

• • •

"Everyone, this is Dario de Luca. He's Marco's brother, and he helped Marco develop the murrine techniques you'll be learning," Tessa said, trying her best to make sure everyone knew Dario was talented enough to teach the class. "I think you'll be able to learn the skills you need, and he's a great guy. Like his brother, Dario is an expert glassblower. These days he owns a chic destination winery, glass gallery, and restaurant called *Vino e Vetro* in Napa Valley, California."

"We are all so grateful Dario is here, thanks to Tessa and Jax. I'm happy we can carry on with class, even in light of this horrendous tragedy. We want our students to be happy," Abby added. "So now, I'll turn things over to Dario."

"*Ciao.* Hello. Nice to meet you," Dario said, addressing the class. Hearing the word *ciao* made me think of the holey red T-shirt with the word *Ciao* printed on its front in fancy script letters that Marco had worn the night he died. "I am here because I know my brother would have wanted me to continue to teach you his—our—techniques. I will not let you down. Now, I will start with a demonstration."

We watched as Dario pulled out bags of slices of patterned glass canes from his brother's toolbox. One bag contained bullseye designs, similar to what Marco had demonstrated on the first night of class, one was full of flower designs, and another bag was full of slices with letters on them.

"We have several types of murrine to choose from," Dario said, showing us a handful of the pea-sized circular slices.

"What are the letters for?" I asked.

"Oh, you can lay out the letters and pick them up on the glass, like any type of murrine. I use them to add my initials. It's my way of adding a signature to a piece. But for this demonstration, I'll be using the traditional millefiori designs."

"Do I have an assistant?"

Sam stepped forward and shook Dario's hand. "I'm Sam, the head glassblower here. If you need anything, let me know."

"Sure. Sam. We have met, no?" Dario asked, but didn't wait for an answer. Dario handed a bag of flower-patterned glass slices to Sam. "Can you preheat these?" While Sam went to the kiln and set up the murrine, Dario looked at his students.

"Does anyone want to get me a big gather of glass from the furnace on a blowpipe?"

Katia raised her hand, and headed to the furnace, and Vance opened the door for her. She gathered some hot glass from the furnace on the end of a pipe and brought it to Dario, who was sitting at the glassblower's bench, ready to make this shapeless blob of glass into something magnificent. Dario worked quietly, occasionally telling students what he was doing. He started by blowing into the blowpipe, and then capping its mouthpiece with his thumb. A bubble formed in the center of the molten glass sphere on the end of the pipe. Dario picked up a moist piece of newspaper, and holding it in the palm of his hand, cupped the paper around the hot glass while rotating the glass on the blowpipe. Steam rose from the paper as he skillfully formed the glass into a perfect ball.

Katia stepped away when Sam returned to help Dario. He opened the furnace's door each time Dario needed to add glass. The men repeated the process of adding and shaping the glass a few times, with Dario blowing into the tip of the blowpipe to expand the bubble and use the wet newspaper to shape the piece after each addition of glass.

"Are you ready with the murrine?" Dario asked Sam. Sam went to the kiln, the same one we used to cook our pizza on the first night of class. He pulled on a pair of Kevlar gloves, opened the kiln, and pulled out a metal tray covered in an array of murrine. After closing the kiln, Sam brought the tray of hot murrine to the marver and set it down. "We've preheated these slices so when I add them to the vase, they won't break. If they are cold, they might crack."

It was the same with beadmaking. I had to be careful when introducing cold glass into my torch because it could crack from thermal shock, the process of heating up or cooling down too quickly. All of the glass shards in the bottom of the crack-off bucket were evidence of thermal shock, caused by hot glass from the furnace dripping into the cold water, and breaking into a million tiny pieces.

Dario heated the piece in the glory hole, then turned and rolled it across the tray of murrine. As he rolled, the murrine stuck to the glass bubble. After he completed the rotation, the entire piece was covered in hundreds of miniature flowers. It was absolutely magical! Dario continued to shape the vessel until it was a perfect gallon-jug-sized cylinder on the end of the blowpipe. The piece was transferred to a punty so Dario could do some final shaping and then placed in a kiln to cool.

We all applauded as the kiln door was shut. Dario hadn't lost his skills as a glassblower.

"Thank you very much," he said, looking proud, and relieved, that he'd succeeded. "Now, let's work on making canes for beads so you can make miniature versions of the vase."

• • •

As I glanced out the window into the utility yard, I noticed a team of uniformed men walking through the field. A CSI team was scouring the area around the studio and the river. The men waved their metal detectors back and forth across the weeds, as they covered every inch of the slope. I wanted to see what they were doing, but felt I needed to buckle down and participate in class.

Each of us used a unique color combination so we knew whose murrine were whose. By the end of the day, we all had plenty to use to make beads. Except for me. I'd been unable to gather the courage to pull glass from the furnace, even with Dario's support. He promised me that even if I didn't make any murrine myself, I'd be able to use some of his to make beads. That was reassuring, but I still was feeling low about being such a complete failure at glassblowing.

Late in the afternoon, the sheriff showed up to talk with the class. Abby gathered us into a circle in the hot shop, and Sheriff Poole stood in the center to address us.

"As you know, we have a homicide on our hands. Well, not on our actual hands, but we've had a murder, and we officially call that a homicide. What I'm going to do, just to save time, is I'm going to ask you all some questions, and you're going to answer them, got it?"

We all nodded, and the sheriff did an awkward 360-degree twist to make sure we all agreed.

"Here's what I want to know. Where were each of you the night Marco de Luca died and who were you with?"

"We were in our trailer stringing necklaces," Sara and Lara said in unison.

"Tessa and I were together in my car," I said, deciding not to raise his ire by reminding him that he already knew our whereabouts that night.

"I was in my tent. Sorry, no one can vouch for me," Vance said.

"I walked with Katia down to the motel. We were together until we got to our rooms. I was alone after that, but don't know about her." Duke said, nodding his head toward Katia, who quietly added that she, too, was alone that night.

"Did anyone see anything unusual the night of the murder?" the sheriff asked.

"I saw a car speed away from the studio, but I can't tell you more than that. It was dark and rainy, and I didn't have my glasses on," Vance said.

I stood quietly and said nothing. It was likely the car Vance had seen was mine. I was fairly certain the figure we had seen thrashing around in the bushes next to the studio was Vance. When Vance approached us at the riverside wrapped in his tarp the day we found Marco's body, he looked a lot like the cloaked figured we'd seen the first night. I decided to keep quiet, and hoped Tessa would, as well. I didn't want the sheriff to decide Tessa and I were suspects, and I didn't want him to consider Vance to be one either. I couldn't be one hundred percent certain he wasn't the killer, since he had been alone during the moments before Tessa saw Marco dead in the studio. Since Vance was one of the sweetest men I'd ever met, it was hard to imagine he was a killer. On the other hand, Vance would have been strong enough to drag Marco into the river that night to get rid of the body, with no one but the Twins nearby as witnesses. But what would have been his motive?

"As you may know, the victim was stabbed to death. The CSI team has located the murder weapon and I'm going to show it to you now. Perhaps one of you can identify it for me." Sheriff Poole reached into a nylon bag at his feet and pulled out a plastic zippered evidence bag with a long kitchen knife in it.

"Does anyone recognize this knife?" he asked. I shut my eyes and evaluated my options. I knew I hadn't killed Marco, but the sheriff didn't know that. Slowly, I raised my hand. If I didn't admit it was my knife, someone would tell the sheriff it belonged to me, and then I'd be in hot water, hotter water than I'd be in if I admitted it myself.

"It's mine," I said.

"I think you better come with me," Sheriff Poole said, grabbing me harshly by the wrist and pulling me out the door toward his car, while the rest of the class stood aghast, silently watching the sheriff drag me away.

"Where are we going? Are you arresting me?"

"I'm taking you in for questioning," the sheriff replied.

"Tessa! Help me!"

"I know exactly what to do," Tessa said, as she gave me a double thumbs-up.

SEVENTEEN

THE SHERIFF'S STATION was bleak with its gray walls, matching floor, and short row of cramped cells. The first cell was painted a hideous drunk tank pink. I was certain Dez had spent some time in the bubble gum colored cell. I hoped I wasn't about to get thrown in there, too, and not only because of its bright color, which I noticed was nearly the same shade as Val's vibrant pink sofa.

Sheriff Poole sat me down in the guest chair next to his desk. "It's my lunchtime. I hope you don't mind if I eat," he said, pulling a fat sandwich out of a crumpled bag, the words *Meat and Eat* in bold letters across its front. He clearly didn't believe in deconstructing his enormous sandwich before trying to eat it, as we had done. I was surprised to see he could open his mouth wide enough to take a bite, but maybe not that surprised. I sat there looking at him, suddenly hungry. I hadn't eaten since the breakfast Dario made this morning, but it was clear the sheriff wasn't going to share. I tried hard not to look as pathetic as Gumdrop sometimes does when I'm eating and he's hungry, of course, he's always hungry, but never for the crunchies in his bowl.

"Why am I here?"

"Because the knife, the murder weapon, belongs to you."

"I don't deny it's my knife. I used it to cut Tessa's birthday cake," I said.

"The weapon was here the night of the murder."

"There were all sorts of sharp objects around the night of the murder."

"The knife had your fingerprints all over it."

"Because it's my knife!" I said, slamming my hand down on the desk.

"It just so happens the DNA from that EYE-talian guy is on the blade."

"How do you know that?"

"I'm the one asking the questions right now. Let's get down to business. Why don't you tell me what happened on Friday night," the sheriff said, clicking his pen and starting to write.

"I saw you on Friday night, remember? I was at the car repair shop with Tessa. We called 911! How could we be the murderers?"

"You shut your mouth and keep it shut. Now, tell me about what led you to kill Marco de Luca."

I said nothing.

"Well? Well?"

"You told me to shut my mouth. I didn't kill Marco de Luca."

"Oh, so your friend Tessa, maybe she's the culprit? She was out of your sight before she discovered the victim."

"She was never out of my sight and even if she was, she was gone for only a second before returning, not long enough to have killed anyone. She is far too petite to have overpowered a man of his size and strength."

"I think you should fess up and then we can process your paperwork. Maybe I need to put you in a cell for a little while. Let you think about what you've done. Then maybe you'll be ready to tell me what happened." Sheriff Poole took another bite of sandwich. A chunk of onion fell onto the desk. He scooped it up and pushed it into his mouth.

"I've got nothing to confess…" I closed my eyes, and tried to pull myself together.

"I know you're feeling guilty. Are you gonna cry? Terrible

business, killing someone like you did."

I opened my eyes and glared at the piggish sheriff.

"Am I under arrest? Because if I'm not, I'd like to leave," I said.

"No, I've not arrested you—yet, but you'll leave when I'm ready for you to leave. It's a long walk back to Carthage. Besides, you bolting out of here is going to make you look mighty guilty."

He finished his sandwich, licked the tips of each finger, wiped his mouth, and burped. What a classy guy. The door opened behind me. I twisted around to see who it was, hoping Tessa had come to rescue me.

Instead, I stared slack-jawed at Ryan Shaw standing in the doorway. *What the heck was he doing here?*

"Hello," Ryan glanced at the sheriff's badge. "Sheriff Poole. I'm Ryan Shaw, Seattle P.D." Ryan did not look my way.

"Nice to meet ya," the sheriff said, shaking Ryan's hand. "You can call me Harvey. We're pretty casual out here."

"And what are you doing with this young lady?" Ryan got two points for calling me a young lady.

"Interrogating this suspect. Her fingerprints are all over the murder weapon used in the homicide of that EYE-talian man over at the glassblowing place," the sheriff said.

"That's because it's my knife! I dropped it the other night," I said, glancing up at Ryan, who still didn't address me directly, but instead kept his gaze leveled on the Sheriff Poole.

"You're aware of section RF-328 sub-section B of the King County inter-jurisdictional guidelines?" Ryan asked the sheriff.

"Of course, I am. I'm not some sort of yokel, you know. I know the laws, even that RF-32…uh, you know the rest," the sheriff said.

"Then you know I have authority to take this individual for interrogation at our HQ."

"Well, I, of course, but, then—" Harvey sputtered.

"I've got the release papers right here." Ryan pulled a sheaf of papers from his leather notebook.

"Fine. Take her," Harvey said, defeated.

Ryan returned the papers to his book, grabbed me roughly under one arm, and pulled me to a standing position.

"You better not try to escape, miss." He pulled me toward the door.

Ryan had never called me miss before.

"Oh, no, officer, I promise to stay right here by your side," I said.

"And Harvey, I'm sure you know you need to complete transfer form AD-794."

"Of course, I'll get that done right away."

"What the heck is going on? Can you let go of me? You're hurting my arm," I said, once we were in the parking lot next to Ryan's police car. I yanked my arm out of his grip.

"Please, miss, you need to get in the back," Ryan said, looking over his shoulder at Sheriff Poole peering out the window at us. He opened the back door of his cruiser, put his hand on my head and pushed me into the car, slamming the door behind me.

Dazed, I sat in the back seat of the patrol car, which looked like a normal car except for two unique features. There were no door handles or window controls, and there was heavy-duty mesh between the front seat and the back to keep criminals like me from escaping.

"Dammit, Ryan! What's going on?"

Without a word, he put the car in gear and headed down the narrow road away from the police station. Ryan found a quiet side street and pulled over. He got out of the car and opened the rear door, an unusually stern look on his face.

"Would you like to get out of the back seat, miss?" Ryan couldn't contain himself any longer and burst out laughing.

"Can you please tell me what's going on here, because I am very confused," I said, pulling myself out of the back seat and landing a little too close to Ryan. "And stop calling me miss!"

"I'm transferring—"

"Yes, I know, with some complicated form,"

"That doesn't, in fact, exist."

"I saw the papers, you nearly handed them to him."

"Nearly. If he'd taken them, he'd have discovered that they were printouts of the parking citations I gave last week."

"There's no RF dash whatever it is?"

"No, Jax, there's not."

"You! Big! Liar!" I said hitting him on the shoulder with each word. "Harvey's going to be pissed off when he finds out you stole his prize suspect—me!"

"I don't think he'll find out. We had a pretty convincing show when I jammed you into the back seat."

"That was one smooth rescue mission there," I said, pulling myself up to sit on the hood of the car.

"I couldn't see you getting thrown in the drunk tank." He faced me, his knees now pressed against mine. "I want to apologize for so many things, for that ticket I gave Tessa, for being out of touch since I moved here. I've been trying to make a good impression, working extra hours when I can, attending all the in-service training."

"It's okay, I understand," I said, although I remained a little peeved that he had given Tessa a ticket only a few days before.

"So, what happens now? Are you going to take me into custody?"

"No, I thought I'd kiss you." He bent forward and lightly kissed my lips. I felt my neck flush red. I was pretty sure that was not the most attractive way to blush, but it was all I had, and given all the other ways my body betrayed me on a regular basis, it wasn't so bad.

"So, no custody for me, then?" I said, releasing him before things got too hot and heavy here on the hood of a Seattle P.D. sedan.

"Why? Did you do something illegal?"

"No! Did Tessa get ahold of you?"

"No, but I was…"

"You were what?"

"Already out here," Ryan said, a note of embarrassment in his voice.

"We are *way* outside of Seattle. This can't be part of your beat. Did you follow me?" Ryan had followed me once before, trying to keep me out of harm's way when I was looking for a mysterious woman on the streets of Portland late one night a few months ago. "Well? Did you?"

"I was only trying to keep you safe," Ryan said, an earnest smile on his face—on his handsome, irresistible face. Then I recalled the ticket he gave Tessa and the time he pulled us over to apologize. I pushed him back and slid off the hood of the car.

"We're done here. Thanks for the rescue and all, but seriously, it really creeps me out that you'd be stalking me out here in the boondocks."

"Stalking is a pretty strong word, Jax."

"Fine. Call it what you want. I don't like being followed. It's like you don't trust me to take care of myself. And I assure you—"

"It's only because I care," Ryan said, grabbing me by the forearm as I turned away.

"You want to know how you can show you care? By calling me on the phone. Send me a text, maybe with a cute little heart emoji sometime." I yanked my arm out of his grip. "Can you please take me back to the studio?"

Wordlessly, we both got in his car. This time, I rode in the front seat. He took me back to Old Firehouse Studio.

"Thanks for the ride," I said, as he pulled up to the studio.

"You're welcome. Stay out of trouble, will you?"

"It's not like I mean to get into trouble."

"Try and listen to Tessa a little more. I don't want to rescue you again."

"You didn't need to rescue me. I had things under control!" I glanced up as a dark government-issue sedan parked a few yards away. Oh, dear. It was Zachary.

"Zachary! Wow, I—" I said as he got out of the car and headed toward me.

"Tessa called me. She said you were in trouble and needed my help, but it looks like you got a better offer," Zachary said.

"No, I—he—" I said using my most eloquent words. Ryan got out of the car and came around to meet Zachary between the two sedans.

"I happened to be on patrol, and happened to be on hand to help Jax," Ryan said, puffing himself up a bit to stand a little taller than Zachary. Zachary stared back at him silently and then focused on me.

"Zachary, I didn't ask him to come. He showed up," I said, and then realized I was not being considerate of Ryan, who after all, had pulled off a pretty amazing rescue less than an hour ago. "He just happened to be here to help me."

"Happened to be here? Happened to be way out here in the sticks?" Zachary asked, incredulously. "I seriously doubt that. No Seattle officers are assigned this far off the beaten path. Are you even on duty right now, Officer Shaw?"

"With all due respect, sir, you are not my superior officer," Ryan said, a tinge of defensiveness in his voice.

"It shouldn't be too hard to find out," Zachary replied, pulling out his phone.

"Guys! I think we should let this go, okay? Ryan, I bet you need to get back on your patrol," I said, although I was actually wondering, now that Zachary had brought it up, whether he was on duty. "And Zachary, I'm fine. I'm thankful Tessa called you, but I really had things under control." Although it was not, strictly speaking, true.

Both men glared at each other, turned, and headed silently toward their cars.

• • •

I found Tessa and the rest of the class in the hot shop making murrine.

"Jax! You're back," Tessa said, jumping up and giving me a hug. "The sheriff let you go."

"I was rescued by Ryan. He sprang me from jail. I need to avoid the sheriff from now on. He thinks Ryan has taken me to Seattle to be interrogated."

"What? I sent Zachary to rescue you," Tessa said.

"I ran into him outside when Ryan dropped me off. That was awkward. Those two definitely don't like each other."

"Or are jealous," Tessa replied.

"Either way, I'm hoping I don't have to endure another meet-and-greet like that one."

In the hot shop, the Twins were stretching a hot glass cane. One stood by the furnace holding a punty while the other was nearly out of the rolling door's opening, pulling the glass with diamond shears. I'd never seen them do anything but string necklaces and say negative and pretentious things, so I was surprised to see them being so competent. After stretching their cane and setting it down on the floor, Dario approached and nipped it up into sections with a tile cutter. He picked up a still-hot piece with tweezers and together we looked at the end of the cane so we could see the design: a skull. Of course.

"Okay, Jax, are you ready to try?" Dario asked, nodding toward the furnace.

"Not really."

"Come now, I will help you. Here is a punty. You hold it like this," he said, placing it in my hands and guiding me toward the furnace. "Sam, can you open the door, just a crack?" Dario stood right behind me and whispered into my ear. "Okay now you take one step forward and now another. Now, you slide the punty into the furnace. Are your eyes open?"

"No."

"*Che casino!*" he said. It was funny to hear someone use this expression other than Tessa. Somehow, I thought it was a phrase only she used. "Well then, open them!"

I did what he said, sliding the punty into the furnace, getting a mass of glass on the end of it, and then pulling it out. A dime-sized blob of glass hung from the tip of the punty.

"Dammit!" I said. "I honestly tried. I swear. I don't think I'm cut out for doing this glassblowing thing."

"We will try again another day."

"I think I'm going to stick to glass beadmaking," I said, crashing the punty into the bucket of water at my feet. The hot glass sizzled and popped off the thick metal rod, the clear rubble mixing in with some colored glass in the bottom of the bucket.

"Ah, yes. I am looking forward to having us all make glass beads on the torches. When do we get to do that?" Dario asked Abby.

"Oh, well, the schedule got thrown off track. I'm not sure when that's going to happen, but we could do it tomorrow, if that works for Tessa." Tessa had agreed to let the students use the torches at her studio during the class, since Abby and Dez's studio didn't have any beadmaking equipment.

"That's great. I'll make sure Fremont Fire is ready for everyone," Tessa said, then gave the students the studio's address.

"Well then, it is settled. Tomorrow we have a field trip to Tessa's studio in Seattle," Dario told the class.

"Are you going to stay at my house again tonight?" I asked Dario.

"No, I can't possibly let you sleep on the sofa for another night. Abby was able to get me a room at the Cascade Corners Motel. Apparently someone checked out, so she reserved a room for me."

I kicked myself for not having checked for vacancies at the motel. I was sure Tessa and Vance felt the same. Vance could have gotten out of the rain, and Tessa and I could have stopped our maddening drive each day. At least I knew I could sleep in my own bed tonight.

Katia smiled a little when she heard the news that Dario was staying at the same motel as she was. She might not have liked Marco, but she seemed smitten with Dario.

"And who can give Dario a ride to Fremont Fire tomorrow?" Abby asked.

"I'll do it," Katia said quickly, before anyone else could volunteer. I'm sure she relished the idea of spending a forty-five minute drive alone in her car with a sexy Italian glassblower.

Violetta wandered into the hot shop from the break room. "May I come to your studio tomorrow to give a presentation about my Venetian beads?" Violetta asked Tessa. "You can invite whomever you like."

"Of course. Do you want some help packing up your beads?" Tessa asked.

"*Grazie*. That would be very nice," Violetta said.

Tessa and I followed Violetta into the break room to help her pack up. She handed us stacks of plastic zippered bags and tissue, and we painstakingly wrapped each strand and put them into plastic bags, then placed them into a rolling suitcase with all the other valuable merchandise. When we were nearly done, Abby called Violetta into her office and left us alone in the break room. Tessa took one of the strands out of a bag.

"You're not seriously thinking of buying that, are you?"

"No. Shhh." Tessa said, untying the strand, removing three beads, pocketing them, retying the strand, and replacing it.

"Did I just watch you steal some beads?" I asked in a whisper.

"Borrow, Jax. Just borrow. I'm sure they're Venetian, but not sure they're old," Tessa said. "Let's get out of here before Violetta comes back and finds she's a few beads short of a strand."

"*You're* a few beads short of strand," I said.

"Are you saying I'm crazy?" Tessa asked.

"Yes, but no crazier than I am."

EIGHTEEN

BACK AT HOME, after our dinner of Chinese takeout, Tessa pulled Violetta's beads from her purse and set them on the kitchen table.

"There's something wrong with these beads," Tessa said.

"You mean other than the fact that their price is astronomical?"

"There's something weird about them. See how they look compared to my nonna's." Tessa rummaged around in her purse and found her grandmother's beads.

"See, they're different," Tessa said, placing the beads side by side.

And they did look different. The colors in Tessa's grandmother's beads were muted, and the shapes of the patterns were more complex than those in the beads she had taken from Violetta. One explanation was simply that the beads were made by different people who had access to different supplies and tools.

"I don't know enough about vintage beads to be able to tell if this set is old," I said picking up Violetta's beads. "But I think I know someone who can help us figure it out."

"Rosie?" Tessa replied.

"Rosie? No. She may sell a lot of new beads, but I don't think she knows much about old ones. We need someone who knows about antiques, not just about beads. We can also hear what he has to say about the whale carving we found in the trunk."

"Who?" asked Tessa.

"Mr. Chu!"

"You're going to ask the crazy cat man?"

"He may be a crazy cat man, but he's also an antiques dealer. I think it may be a package deal along with the cats, you have to own an antiques store."

"We don't have to go into his house, right? I think that would freak me out," Tessa said. She didn't dislike cats. She liked Gumdrop. But even I, loving cats as I much as I did, didn't think I could set foot inside of Mr. Chu's house without feeling a little claustrophobic—or was that cat-strophobic?

I looked out the window toward Mr. Chu's house across the driveway. His lights were on. Silhouettes of two cats crossed back and forth along the sill of his curtained window. Mr. Chu was awake, and I hoped he was willing to accommodate unexpected visitors at such a late hour.

"I know this is a scary thought, but we should go see him," I said. "Now. If these beads are fakes, they might have something to do with Marco's death. If Mr. Chu could help us determine whether the beads were truly old, that might put us on the track of the killer. Think of it as an adventure."

"I know about you and your adventures. Somehow, they always end up with us in trouble," Tessa said.

"I don't know how much more trouble I could get into this week. I've already found a dead body, been accused of murder, taken to jail…"

"Okay, but only if we talk with him on the doorstep. I'm not going in," Tessa said.

As we headed through my studio, I remembered the whale carving in the trunk beneath one of my worktables. Diving under the table, I found the whale carving in the trunk and pulled it from its pouch. Tessa brought the beads from her grandmother and Violetta, and we headed out the back door. She didn't look happy about it and I wasn't too thrilled either, but if it could help us find Marco's killer, it would be worth it.

We walked across the alley and knocked on Mr. Chu's back door. After a few minutes, he opened it a crack.

"What do you want?" he asked.

"Hi, I hope I'm not coming over too late," I said. I felt Tessa standing close behind me.

"Oh, this is Tessa Ricci. Tessa, this is Mr.—"

"All right already," said Mr. Chu impatiently. He was more of a cat person than a people person. "Why are you here bothering me?"

"We want to ask you about some beads," Tessa said, emerging from behind me and holding Violetta's beads out to show him.

"Come in, come in. You can't be standing outside with the door open, some of my cats will escape," Mr. Chu said, beckoning us to come inside. Tessa swallowed hard and peered into his front room. She must have decided it wasn't too scary to enter since she followed me as I headed reluctantly into his home. Mr. Chu closed his robe and shuffled over to his roll-top desk, shooing a cat from a stack of papers. There were cats everywhere. At least twenty, doing the things cats do, mostly sleeping.

Mr. Chu's house was exactly as mine had been before it had been split down the middle. It was a large house, which was a good thing, given the number of cats living there. My miraculous discovery was that even though he had far too many cats, his house didn't smell like a litter box and his furniture wasn't covered in cat hair. He might have had a lot of cats, but he seemed to take good care of them, and that meant I wasn't going to have to call animal services to report a cat-hoarding problem.

"We have a couple of items we were hoping you could tell us something about." I handed the whale carving to Mr. Chu.

He said nothing as he held the miniature sculpture in his weathered hands. He turned on the reading light on his desk and pulled out his loupe.

"Sit, sit," he said. We sat down on his old tweedy couch in spots that were not occupied by cats. A large orange tabby walked over and started sniffing me. He must have smelled Gumdrop, but this didn't stop him from climbing into my lap and proceeding to knead his sharp claws into my thighs. Tessa and I sat quietly, craning our necks to see what Mr. Chu was doing. What could he see that we couldn't?

"What you've got here is quite special. It's an Inuit carving of a whale. Very old. Very valuable. Are you selling?"

"Oh, I'm not interested in selling it. I'd like to know a little more about it," I said. "It was my Great-Aunt Rita's."

"Ah, she was a nice lady. Kept to herself," said Mr. Chu, giving me a squinty look, which seemed to say he'd like it better if I did the same.

"Thanks. That's great." I tucked the tiny whale carving into my pocket.

"What? You're not wrapping that up? I told you it was valuable," Mr. Chu said impatiently. "Give it to me."

I handed the carving to him, and he wrapped it up with some tissue paper. "Keep it safe. It's worth maybe five thousand dollars. Maybe more." Tessa and I looked at each other, dumbstruck. She passed the beads she'd stolen from Violetta to Mr. Chu.

"Can you take a look at these?" Tessa asked.

"Ah, what you've got here are some fakes. Whoever is making these, they're trying to make them look old, but they're off on some things."

"Like what?" I asked.

"The millefiori patterns are all wrong. You don't find work as sloppy as this in the older beads, like this star with so few points. You'll never see that in real old Venetian beads. They tended to have a lot more detail. And the colors, this bright purple, nobody made colors like that until recently."

Mr. Chu passed the beads back to Tessa with a look of disgust. "Just junk."

As Tessa expected, the beads weren't old. She pulled the other strand from her purse and held it out. These were her grandmother's, and she knew for a fact they were antiques.

Mr. Chu took the strand. "Now, this is more like it. These are nice. See the flowers? The patterns are more complex than those others. And the colors, much more basic with no exotic purples." He handed the strand back to Tessa. "Hope you didn't pay too much for the first strand. It's not worth much, but this one, this one's authentic. Worth a lot."

"I appreciate your time and expertise," I said.

"Right, well, good night," Mr. Chu said, ushering us to the door, dodging cats as we went. We walked back across the alley to my back door. Mr. Chu picked up a Siamese and waved its little paw at us. We waved back.

As Tessa had thought, there was something wrong with Violetta's beads. They were fakes. What we needed to know now was whether Violetta knew they were fake and how these strange beads fit into Marco's murder, if they did.

"There's one way we can find out if Violetta knows if the beads are authentic or not. We need someone to confront Violetta about what she is selling and then see how she reacts," I said. "Maybe she'll break down and confess everything. Maybe Marco had given her the beads to sell and had lied to her about them. Maybe she found out they were fakes and he was committing fraud, so she killed him. Maybe—"

"Can you stop with the 'maybes' for a second and slow down that wild imagination of yours?" Tessa asked. "Who are we going to get to be so obnoxious to accuse Violetta of selling cheap imitations? Someone so rude—"

"Rosie!"

"You're right. She could do it," Tessa replied.

NINETEEN

THE FOLLOWING MORNING Tessa and I were up early. Each of us had our own missions for the day. Tessa headed to her studio to get ready for the students who soon would be arriving for a day of beadmaking demonstrations, including Violetta's presentation about vintage beads. Tessa and I both hoped Rosie Paredes, the owner of our local bead shop, would agree to help us with the next part of our plan. We wanted Rosie to come to Tessa's studio to look at the Venetian beads as a potential buyer, and in the process, find out if Violetta had anything to do with the death of Marco de Luca.

I met Rosie last year when she'd hosted an event at her shop, Aztec Beads. Without a doubt, Rosie was the most obnoxious person I'd ever met. She'd be perfect to help us find out whether Violetta knew that what she was selling were counterfeit beads. Rosie could be feisty and was known to be quite temperamental. It had taken some coaching from Tessa to keep Rosie from flying off the handle at the smallest provocation, but she was making good progress at being a patient friend and parent.

Rosie's daughter, Tracy, was behind the counter when I arrived at Aztec Beads.

"Is Rosie here?" I asked.

"Mama's in the classroom pricing some new strands of copper beads," Tracy replied. Tito, their obnoxious Chihuahua-mix dog, growled at me as I passed him. Rosie barely looked up when she saw me weaving my way through the shop, which was so packed with inventory I couldn't move in a straight line. I turned sideways to make sure I didn't knock the boxes of seed beads off the low shelves against the wall.

"Hi, Rosie," I said, sitting down next to her, a giant pile of strands of copper beads in all sizes and shapes in front of her.

"Hi. Sorry. Can't talk now," Rosie said, not pausing for even a second from writing prices on tiny stickers.

"How about I help you price these and in return, you help me with something?" I asked.

Rosie said nothing and continued writing numbers on stickers.

"Rosie?"

Irritated, she finally stopped and looked up at me. I smiled and reached for a pen and some price tags.

"Fine." She handed me what I needed to help her with the pricing. "Mark all of these five dollars." Rosie handed me a pile of beads, and I went to work. Fifteen minutes later, we were done, and Rosie sat there looking at me.

"Thanks for the help," Rosie said. "When I get into the pricing zone it's hard to stop. I don't want to get confused and start marking things wrong."

"I need a favor," I said. Rosie looked at me and blinked.

"I'm not into favors," Rosie said, drumming her stubby fingers on the table.

"What if it helped us catch a killer?"

"That I could handle. After all the chaos last year here at the shop, I nearly died."

"I know, I was there, remember? I saved you from strangulation, I caught a killer."

"Fine. I'll help," Rosie said. "What do I have to do?"

"Just be yourself." In Rosie's case that meant being surly and confrontational, a perfect fit for the job we had for her. I explained what I wanted her to do.

Tessa phoned me. "Everyone is here. Are you coming?"

"We're on our way," I said.

"Are you ready?" I asked Rosie, as I hung up the phone.

"As ready as I'll ever be." She grabbed her long black raincoat and handbag, and we headed toward the front of her shop.

"You're okay to watch things while I'm gone?" she asked her daughter.

"Of course, Mama, go and help them catch a killer."

With Rosie in the Ladybug next to me, we started the short drive to Tessa's studio.

"It's too cold in here," Rosie said, punching the buttons on the heater in the Ladybug. "Does this seat go back any farther?"

I was thankful the drive to the Fremont District was only ten minutes. Much longer in the car with Rosie, and I'd be ready to drop her at the side of the road. The rain was coming down hard again, and I flipped on the wipers.

"Your wipers sure don't work very well," Rosie said.

I gripped the steering wheel tighter, not wanting to say anything for fear of exploding, which was more likely in Rosie's playbook than mine.

When we arrived at Fremont Fire, Violetta was putting her beads on a table that Tessa set up by the front door. I was sure Violetta was excited to get a chance to finally sell some beads this week, since I didn't think she'd sold a single bead to the students in Carthage.

In the back of Tessa's shop, where she had a glass beadmaking classroom, Vance had settled in at a torch and was doing a demonstration on how to create one of his signature glass beads, which looked as if it had been spray-painted with graffiti. The Twins and Katia looked on in interest. Duke was nowhere to be found.

"Thanks so much for coming. Please, have a seat," Violetta said. Rosie sat down at the table and ran her pudgy hands over the strands, saying nothing. "Please, let me know if you have any questions."

"Hmmm," Rosie replied, not looking up from the beads. She

plucked a strand from the pile and ran the tip of a fingernail over the surface of a bead. "Hmmm."

"Those are very nice. Very old," Violetta said.

"How old?"

"Oh, those are at least a hundred years old, possibly older," Violetta said.

"How do you know that?" Rosie asked, in her surliest voice, finally looking Violetta straight in the eye. Tessa and I casually looked toward Violetta to see if we could glimpse any sort of reaction, which could tell us if she knew the truth about these beads.

There was nothing but a smile on Violetta's face. "I know these beads. They came from Marco's family. He said he found them in his nonna's basement."

"They look new to me," Rosie said, keeping up the charade.

"Ah, but the patina—"

"Acid etching is easy," Rosie said, accusing Violetta of using chemicals to make the beads look older than they actually were. "Or maybe someone used a rock tumbler to get this matte finish."

"But you don't often see these rare colors," Violetta said, sounding more and more desperate to convince Rosie that these beads were valuable and legitimate.

"Rare colors? I'd say some of these colors look too modern to be as old as you say they are. This purple, they never made beads in this color," Rosie said, tossing the beads back onto the table. I had told her what little I had learned from Mr. Chu. In reality, she had no idea what colors were old and what were new, but Rosie was on a roll.

"I'm sorry you don't like what you see," Violetta said. "I can assure you these are real Venetian beads from a century ago. Perhaps you'd like to take some time by yourself to look?" Violetta said, grabbing her cigarettes and heading out the door.

"What do you think?" I asked Rosie, once Violetta was out of earshot.

"She thinks they're real, even if they're not," Rosie said. "That's my gut reaction."

"I think so, too. She seems to be earnest about what she's selling," I said. "Mr. Chu could be wrong. The beads truly could be old. What do you think, Tessa?"

"She's a liar."

TWENTY

"HOW DO YOU KNOW?" I asked.

"What do you know about Venice?" Tessa answered my question with a question.

"It's the most important city in the world for glass, other than Seattle," I said. "And it's full of canals, built on a lagoon…"

"Right. She said Marco had found these beads in the basement of his nonna. I've got news for you: There are no basements in buildings in Venice, only water and pillars that hold the buildings up. She knows the beads are fake," Tessa said.

"She's lying about where they came from?" Rosie asked.

"Or Marco was lying about where they came from," I said.

"That's a good point. Maybe he made them, treated them with chemicals to make them look old, and passed them off to Violetta to sell," Tessa said. "They could have been in this scam together."

"So, now what? Am I supposed to buy some of these beads? Because they're a real rip-off," Rosie said.

"Exactly. A real rip-off. And now we need to figure out who was ripping off whom," I said.

Violetta returned from her cigarette break.

"Thanks for showing me your beads. I can't buy them right now.

Outside my budget," Rosie said, abruptly standing and heading for the door.

"*Scusi*? May I speak to you, Tessa?" Violetta said with tears in her eyes.

"I need to get back to the shop." Rosie stood in the doorway, hands on her hips, with no patience for crying or comforting.

I dropped Rosie off and headed back to Tessa's studio. While I didn't mind missing Violetta's presentation about vintage glass beads, I did want to see Dario's demonstration using some of the murrine we made over the last few days, that is, the murrine everyone else had made.

There were envelopes with students' names on them in the middle of the table. Each was filled with slices of pattern cane, murrine we could use today while we made beads. I grabbed my envelope and poured its contents on the worktable. Instead of brightly colored flower patterns, all that were in my envelope were murrine with letters on them.

I called Tessa over.

"Very funny, Tessa. Did you do this?"

"No. I picked up the envelopes from Abby and brought them here. Why is yours full of letters?"

"I haven't been able to make any canes. I'm the remedial student, remember? This must be some joke. Or maybe it's a message from Marco's killer. Well, we certainly need to try and decipher it." I said, moving murrine around. "How about this?"

NUDE EXIT

"Plus, I've got a couple of letters left over," I added.

"No," Tessa said, scrambling the letters up again. "Let's see. I was always pretty good at these games when I was younger." Tessa slid the last letters into place and gasped.

YOU DIE NEXT

"Maybe it's a message from the killer. Whoever it is, they're trying to scare me," I said. "It's not going to work. They're probably hoping I'll go home and not come back to class." While that was tempting, I was going to finish this class, and blow some glass, if it was the last thing I did. And if the murderer got his or her way, it would be the last thing I did.

"Okay, everyone, gather around," Dario said, as he sat at one of the torches in Tessa's studio. He held a few thin murrine slices in his hand. "I'm going to show you how to make a glass bead in the torch and add these murrine to it." He started by lighting the torch. He melted a long rod of black glass in the torch's flame, then wrapped the glass around the mandrel, a metal wire coated in a clay-like substance on its tip. After applying the glass to the mandrel, he used a small graphite paddle to shape the glass into an oval bead.

"Now, I'll pick up a chip of murrine and gently heat it, then I'll press it onto the bead," Dario said, holding the murrine in tweezers and waving it in the torch's flame, attaching it to the bead, then using the graphite paddle to smooth out the chip. Fascinated, we watched as he continued adding murrine to the bead until it was entirely covered in tiny flower designs. "Now, I am finished and will put the bead in the kiln to anneal."

As Dario put it in the kiln, we all applauded the completion of the perfect miniature work of glass art.

"Now, everyone, please light up a torch and practice the skills I have demonstrated for you."

I decided to head home since I had no murrine of my own other than the ones that formed a death threat, which I might make a fun bead with—someday—if I lived long enough.

Coming into my studio, I found Gumdrop curled on top of the quilts in the trunk Tessa and I had pulled out of the attic a few days before. In my haste to grab the ivory whale carving, I must've left the lid to the trunk open. He looked up at me as I sat next to the trunk. I gave him some long strokes down his back.

"Okay, Gummie, what can you tell me?" I picked up the fat gray cat and held him in my lap. He sent me exactly zero psychic vibrations, not even his usual "yellooo." I have always thought my cat was psychic, ever since he'd advised me to move to Seattle. Of course, I'd been ready for a change, and leaving Miami behind was the best decision I'd ever made. While my cat was never helpful in any other way, I was still grateful he'd helped me make my decision to move. And even though I missed my parents and my sister Connie, who still lived in Miami, I was happy to be here in Seattle in this home I'd inherited from my great-aunt. I looked at the quilts in the trunk. There was one for my brother Andy, who already told me he didn't want his. But what about Connie's quilt? I called her.

"Well, hello, stranger," Connie said when she answered her phone. She must've recognized my number. "It's my long-lost sister."

"Sorry. I guess I should call more often. How are you and Jeremy?" Connie's son, Jeremy, was a talented painter. Many of his watercolors graced the walls of my house. The sun-drenched scenes helped keep the place warm and bright even on the coldest, wettest days.

"Oh, we're fine. Jeremy's painting up a storm. He wants to come and visit you this summer. There's an art program he'd like to attend at the University of Washington, but it's a little pricey. It's hard to afford many extracurricular activities as a single parent. I'm hoping to become a partner at the firm this year. That should help."

"I'd love to have him come. He can stay with me, as long as he doesn't mind sharing his room with a bunch of beads," I said, thinking about how packed with beads the Bead Lair was and wondering if an attic renovation was in my future. "I found a quilt in my attic. It's one of Great-Aunt Rita's, and apparently, she wanted you to have it. Your name is pinned to it."

"Oh," Connie said. This was a less than enthusiastic reaction to this gift from our great-aunt. "Do you want it? I've been clearing out all sorts of stuff from my house. Trying to live a little lighter, you know? The last thing I need is a quilt."

"Sure. I get it. I can find a good home for it. It's something that was supposed to be for you. I didn't want to take it, since it was your inheritance."

"Pshhh. I'm not jealous, but you're the one who got the inheritance, right? You got the house."

"Geez, sorry! It's not like I asked for the house."

"I didn't want the house, I didn't need the house. Aunt Rita clearly thought you did. I deal with contentious inheritance issues all the time. They can tear a family apart." Connie was a real estate attorney in Florida. I was certain that in addition to dealing with gullible buyers of prime oceanfront parcels that turn out to be alligator-infested swamps, she also dealt with properties that had ended up in probate when one of her aging clients passed away. "I truly am glad you have the house. No hard feelings, I promise. Anyway, please, enjoy the quilt, and I'll enjoy my clutter-free house."

As I finished the phone call with my sister, I recalled that Dario told Tessa and me his parents had both died in the last couple of years, and that he and Marco were finalizing their parents' estate and preparing to divide the assets. Could Dario have been angry about having to share the family's assets with Marco? Could Dario be his brother's killer? I called Connie back.

"I don't talk with you for months, and now I get two calls in the span of ten minutes," Connie said.

"Sorry. I promise I will call more often. How hard would it be to check the probate records in California for an Italian family?"

"Not too hard. A lot of the information is public. I can do some checking for you." I gave Connie the details on the de Luca brothers.

"Thanks. I owe you one."

"Don't worry. You'll be helping a lot by letting Jeremy stay with you this summer."

I wandered out to the kitchen after we said our good-byes and dropped some crunchies into Gumdrop's bowl. He looked down at the bowl and then up at me. He was waiting. I knew what he wanted.

"Okay, okay. I'm trying to cut back on your catnip consumption, remember?" I told him. Gummie looked down at his bowl and back up at me again, waiting patiently, well, not that patiently. As soon as I opened the freezer, he knew I'd caved in. He stood back from his bowl, ready to make a running jump. I plopped the catnip-infused ice cube into his bowl and he dived in, sending little bits of crunchy cat food flying. I hoped he'd eat some of the kibble at some point, because cats can't live on catnip alone. Maybe it was good he wasn't eating much. Gummie could stand to lose a few pounds, but then again, so could I.

I was a little hungry and didn't have much to eat in the house, so I decided to see if Val had anything she was willing to share. As I pulled open my front door, I glimpsed the back of a man's dark overcoat slipping inside Val's door, before it was hastily shut behind him.

That must have been Val's mystery man. Her secrecy about the identity of her guest had piqued my curiosity. I knocked on my neighbor's door. No answer. I pounded on her door.

"I know you're in there, you might as well open up." The door opened a crack. Val's heavily mascaraed eye squinted at me.

"What do you want?" Val whispered.

"I want to know what's going on in there."

"Don't be so nosy."

"Me—nosy? You're the queen of nosy! Come on, who's in there?"

"It's a secret."

"You know all of my secrets. Right? And you always tell me everything. You tell me more than I ever want to know!"

"I've been sworn to secrecy!"

"Val, it's not like I've got anyone to tell."

"You've got Tessa."

"But she's the most trustworthy person in the world. And so am I."

"Fine," Val said, opening her front door enough for me to slip inside before she shut and locked it behind me. Sitting on Val's bright pink sofa with zebra-print pillows was rock superstar Freddie "Boom Boom" Roberts, looking a little worse for wear. He was one of the best old-school American guitarists born in the heartland of the good old U. S. of A. He'd been touring pretty much continuously since the 1970s.

I stood in the entryway, stunned.

"Now you know," said Val, collapsing into a kitchen chair. Apparently, keeping this big secret from me had been tremendously stressful for her.

"Uncle Freddie, this is my neighbor, landlord, and number-one gal pal, Jax O'Connell," she said, grabbing one of my hands and pulling me toward her uncle, as Freddie stood up and extended his hand. "And Jax, this is my Uncle Freddie. My dad's brother."

I was immediately hit by one thing: Freddie, though he always seemed like a rock-n-roll giant when I saw him in music videos, was, in fact, not much taller than me. It was hard to believe he was from the same gene pool as Val, who towered above us both, even when she wasn't wearing high heels. One thing Freddie and Val did have in common was a love of tall hair, although it was entirely likely that Freddie's was enhanced by hair plugs.

"Wow, it's super to meet you," I said shaking his hand. The shaking part was easy, since I was already trembling all over. This was all a little hard to wrap my head around. What was Freddie Roberts doing here? This was going to be my only opportunity to ask, so I decided to plunge in. I took a seat on an overstuffed zebra-striped ottoman near Freddie. "What brings you to Seattle?"

"I'm in town trying to find a new place to live. My old lady, that is, ex-old-lady, she got the mansion in the Hamptons. I can't live in Aspen all year long. I need to find some place where people will leave me alone, but you know, is close to a cool place like Seattle. And I'm looking for some new business opportunities. I can't keep doing this rock thing until I'm eighty. My agent's already booking me into some of the smaller clubs and the county fairs. It's time to hang it up real soon."

"And why are you staying here with Val?" I asked.

"I'm trying to stay out of the public eye right now. Going in and out of a hotel every day, it ends up drawing attention to me. I'm trying to lie low."

"It's amazing to meet you. I'm sorry to have forced my way in. Your secret is safe with me," I said.

"Hope to see you again. Any friend of my little Valerie is a friend of mine."

I didn't know which of these facts was more shocking: I was now a friend of rock-n-roll great Freddie Roberts, or that he called Val "his little Valerie."

Val ushered me to the door. "You should come back over tomorrow. Keep it quiet. Don't tell anyone Uncle Freddie is here. We don't want the house to get mobbed."

"Not even Tessa?"

"Not even Tessa!"

I slipped out the door and realized I'd left without any snacks. I turned to knock again, but before I could, Val opened the door and shoved a plate of cupcakes at me.

"Thank you!" I said.

"I'm buying your silence with these, got it?"

"Got it." Some people get hush money. I get hush desserts.

TWENTY-ONE

MY PHONE RANG, and I answered.

"Jax, it's Zachary. I'm in the neighborhood, and I have too much pizza."

"You realized that after you ordered it?"

"They messed up my order, so they gave me a free one. Not that I need to explain—"

"Are you inviting yourself over?"

"I don't have to stay. I can drop off the pizza, if you're busy—"

"I'm only giving you a hard time. You know, like sometimes you give me. Come on over, and I'll tell you what I've learned. Plus, I've got dessert," I said, setting the plate of chocolate cupcakes with pink frosting on my kitchen counter.

I was glad Zachary was coming to visit. I could fill him in on what I'd discovered about Violetta and the beads, and perhaps even explain why he'd found me getting out of Ryan Shaw's police car in Carthage. I wasn't looking forward to that part of the conversation.

• • •

"The beads are fakes. They're not old or valuable," I said, as I stuffed the cardboard pizza box into the recycle bin. I explained to Zachary how Mr. Chu had verified that the beads Violetta had been trying to sell were new and how Tessa had caught Violetta in a lie about where the beads came from. "If Violetta was lying about the age and source of the beads, she's committing fraud—selling new beads as antiques. Maybe that's a motive for murder?"

"In all my years on the force, no one has ever been killed over a simple strand of beads," Zachary said.

"You don't understand, antique beads are worth hundreds of dollars. A large collection can be worth thousands. With anything of value, if someone thinks they've been ripped off, they could want to settle the score."

"You think she could have discovered that the beads were fake and turned on Marco?"

"Maybe, or that Marco was going to expose her as a fraud, and Violetta killed him to keep him quiet."

"She is certainly someone we can bring in for questioning, although the sheriff should be the one who does the initial interrogation."

"It shouldn't be a problem for Sheriff Poole. He seems to get a great deal of pleasure from dragging people off to jail," I said. "You know I didn't have anything to do with this murder, right?"

"I'm sure you didn't murder anyone, but you managed to get mixed up in it, again. Tell me this: Why would Sheriff Poole think you murdered Marco de Luca?"

"He found a knife I accidentally dropped outside the studio. He said it had my fingerprints on it," I said.

"That makes sense, it was your knife."

"Exactly! That's what I told him. He also said it had Marco's DNA on it."

"That doesn't make sense. The only DNA testing facility in the area is right here in Seattle, and I can guarantee we haven't run any DNA samples on this case."

"The sheriff is lying?"

"He most certainly is."

"Why is he after me? I didn't do anything wrong!"

"I think he was hoping to get you to confess by bluffing you with his DNA lie," Zachary said.

"Ha! Well, I'm glad he didn't trick me—"

"But now he's on the warpath. He found out what your boyfriend Officer Shaw..."

"Not my boyfriend."

"He tricked the sheriff and spirited you away."

"And how would the sheriff have found that out? The only other person I know who might have told him was you," I said.

"I can assure you—"

"Did you tell Sheriff Poole about Ryan's stunt?" I asked.

"No, but uh...ahem," Zachary paused and cleared his throat. "I did mention in a report that you were still under investigation, due to a procedural error involving a certain newbie officer. Those reports are available to any senior staff member at the Seattle P.D."

"I didn't enlist Ryan to come out and help me," I said.

"Your friend has gotten himself into quite a lot of trouble, actually."

"What?"

"Oh yes, it looks like he had no business being there in Carthage. He threw some bogus forms around. He was already a provisional hire, and with this incident, he may be suspended."

"That's terrible! Can you help him?" I asked.

"Now, why would I want to do that?"

"Because he was helping me. Because he's a nice guy, even if he is a little over-zealous some—well, most—of the time."

"There's not much I can do, but I promise if I can figure out a way to help him, I will."

"Are you jealous?"

"Hm. Well, I wouldn't say that, exactly, but, you know, I'm not always that able, that uh...ahem...eloquent." Zachary cleared his throat again. "I should go, it's getting late." Zachary headed for the door.

"It was great to see you," I said, opening the door for him.

Val trotted out her front door, nearly knocking Zachary over. She had on her brightest pink sweat suit ensemble and glittering white tennis shoes. Behind her, Stanley was anxiously trying to get out the door.

"Well, hello! I'm Val Roberts," she said thrusting her hand at Zachary, while Stanley ran in circles around her, tangling her in his leash.

He grasped her hand and gave it a gentlemanly shake. "How do you do, Val. I'm Zachary."

Val was speechless. I was ready to call the media, because this was big news: Val had run out of words. But Stanley had not run out of things to say and let loose a loud "ah-roo!" Val snapped out her daze long enough to say, "Bye!" as Stanley dragged her down the front steps for his evening stroll-n-poop.

"You have the most unusual life," Zachary said. "What you do for a living, your neighbor, your cat."

"I'm sort of a package deal. Along with me, you get all the rest of the crazies."

"I like this crazy in particular," he said, touching my cheek. "You've got some tomato sauce right here."

What a sweet moment that was, spoiled by a pizza topping.

He pulled out a cloth handkerchief from this pocket and handed it to me. As delicately as possible, I wiped the sauce away. "How's that?"

"Good. Very good." He pulled me close and kissed me. "How's that?"

"Good, I mean, *great*," I said. "I could stand here on the porch all night."

"Ah, well, I can't. I've got work in the morning," Zachary said.

"I'm headed back out to Carthage for another day of class tomorrow morning," I said. "Unless another dead body shows up."

"In which case, you'll stay far, far away, right? Don't make me call Tessa so she can rein you in."

"No reining needed. Thanks for the pizza."

"You are most welcome." He kissed me again and whispered in my ear. "Good night." My heart skipped a beat, maybe two.

Back inside, I heard someone tapping on my back door. I hurried to the door, and found Tessa waiting there for me.

"Why are you so flushed?" she asked.

"I rushed to let you in."

"I'm not sure I believe you," Tessa said, setting her handbag down on the counter and giving me an inquisitive look with a raised eyebrow. "Spill it."

"You're never going to believe what just happened on my doorstep."

"Were you kissing the stern detective?"

"Yes, but—"

"What's in your hand? Did he give you his hankie?"

"He didn't actually give it to me. I think it was more of a loan," I said, placing it on the counter. "What did you learn from Violetta?"

"She said as soon as she told Rosie that the beads came from Marco's nonna's basement, she realized it could not have been true. There would never be a basement in Venice. She said she'd always trusted Marco, and she believed that the beads were old. Now she doesn't know what to believe and has no way of knowing whether she should even be trying to sell them."

"I take it she didn't confess to murdering Marco? Or having been involved in a plot to scam innocent people by selling them bogus beads?"

"Nope. But she said she wanted to get out of here. She's leaving for Italy tomorrow," Tessa said.

"We've got to stop her. She can't leave. She's a suspect!"

"Is she?"

"Of course! She was in Carthage the night Marco died. She had a motive. Marco obviously lied to her about the source of her so-called vintage beads. If she had discovered the lie, that could have made her angry enough to seek revenge. There may be more we don't understand about their shady business dealings," I said.

"I don't know, Jax, but it seems to me there are many other suspects who are more likely than Violetta. For one thing, I don't know how she could have been strong enough to overpower and stab Marco, let alone carry him down to the river and toss him in."

"True. There are other suspects, and I'm sure Sheriff Poole would love to talk to every single one of them. Speaking of which, Ryan Shaw is in deep doo-doo for saving me from the clutches of that disgusting sheriff."

"How did he end up in such trouble?"

"I think Zachary let the Seattle P.D. know Ryan was out of bounds—literally and figuratively."

TWENTY-TWO

IN THE MORNING, as Tessa and I headed through my studio on our way to the car, I made a detour to the bead trays I kept by the back wall. I grabbed one of my ocean beads for Tony Stein, slid it into a plastic bag, and put it in my handbag. I needed to remember to stop by his garage and give him the bead I owed him.

Soon we were on the road headed back out to Old Firehouse Studio. The long trip each day was exhausting, and each mile I drove made me wish we had stayed in Carthage. Of course, there was a killer on the loose in Carthage, so staying away from there as much as possible was probably good for our life expectancies.

We joined the other students in the hot shop, and I couldn't help but notice how Katia was behaving. While she had been cold to Marco, she seemed to be warming up to Dario, and not because the temperature in the room was rising from all the hot glass being used. I could see what she saw in him and how he was more appealing than Marco. While Marco had a slick, cocky attitude, complete with over-the-top overtures toward women, Dario was suave and more of a gentleman.

"Dario," Katia said, calling him over to her. "I'm having trouble clipping these canes. Can you help?" He slid up next to her and took the glass nippers. As he did, her hands rested on his a bit longer than was absolutely necessary. Was a little romance blooming right here in the glass studio? I hoped seeing this wouldn't stir up any feelings that Tessa once had for Dario, although from what Tessa had said, I didn't think those emotions had ever been very strong.

Tessa was busy talking with Abby, who looked like she hadn't slept in days. She was sitting at the back of the hot shop running her hands through her hair over and over. Eventually Abby left to take a phone call and Tessa joined me.

"Poor Abby. She's worried about Dez," Tessa said.

"But I thought going on a bender was a usual thing for him," I said.

"Yes, but Abby said it's strange for him to be gone for so long."

"Want to hit some bars?" I asked Tessa as we watched the other students work.

"It's a little too early for a drink, don't you think?"

"We should try to find Dez. Obviously, Sheriff Poole hasn't had any luck. Let's go check out the local pubs. Maybe we'll find a bartender or barfly who's willing to tell us if they've seen him."

I pulled out my phone and searched for bars in the area. There were exactly two within a ten-mile radius.

"Which would you like to try first, Herbie's Hideaway or the Office?" I asked.

"The Office? What a weird name for a bar."

"It's so you can say, 'Sorry, honey, I had to stay late at the Office.'" When I lived with Jerry in Miami, I heard that line a lot. He spent most of his evenings at a place called the Gym. He could say he stopped at the Gym, which sounded like he was being healthy when in fact, he was pickling his liver in whiskey with beer chasers. "So, which would you like to hit first?"

"Let's go to the Office."

"A respectable choice."

• • •

As we drove to The Office, I thought about the students in class today. Duke was not at Tessa's studio yesterday, and I didn't see him at Firehouse Studio today. Why hadn't he returned to class after hearing that Dario replaced Marco as our instructor? I wondered what he knew about Marco and Dario and their relationships to all the other people in the class this week.

The Office was at the end of a once-paved road. These days it was more like gravel with patches of asphalt here and there, evidence of futile attempts to fix the crumbling road.

"Keep your eyes open for the sheriff," I told Tessa. "I don't want to run into him. If I do, this time I'm sure I'll end up in jail, and I don't think I can count on Ryan saving me again."

"Should we act like we're drunk when we arrive?" Tessa asked. "People might be more willing to talk with us if we were."

"That's a good idea. We can try. Maybe you should try to act a little slutty," I suggested.

"Me? I'm a mom! I don't do slutty! You have more curves than me anyway, why don't you show off a little more cleavage?" She reached over and popped the top button on my blouse. I smacked her hand away. "Excuse me! I am showing off plenty of cleavage already."

I parked the Ladybug behind The Office.

As we stepped inside, it took us a moment for our eyes to adjust to the dim lighting. The bar had the acrid smell of stale beer and cigars. The floor felt sticky as we walked, likely from years of spilled beer and questionable janitorial skills. The place was empty except for the bartender. So much for chatting up the locals.

Tessa and I took seats at the bar. The bartender, lazing behind the beer taps, asked us what we wanted.

"Two beersh, pleash," said Tessa with a fake slur. She swayed a little from side to side.

"Don't go overboard with the drunk thing," I whispered to Tessa.

"You gals want the special lager?"

"Sure," I replied. Tessa continued swaying back and forth. I clamped my hand on the back of her neck to steady her.

The bartender placed the drinks in front of us.

"I haven't seen you two here before."

"Us? We're, um, looking at real estate. Thinking about buying."

Tessa hiccuped in agreement.

I stomped on her foot to get her to tone down her drunken charade.

"We're thinking about moving to Carthage," I said.

"Our friend Dez, he's got a business there," Tessa said. She still sounded drunk but had toned down the slur.

"Dez, yeah. Comes here a lot," the bartender said.

"Nice place. I could see why he'd want to come here," I said looking around at the greasy faux wood paneling and animal head trophies hanging crookedly on the walls. "He talks about this place all the time and said we needed to come check it out."

"We've been here a long time. And Dez, he's the best, one of our most loyal customers."

"He said we could come here almost any night and find him," I said.

"Oh, yeah, he's put away a swimming pool worth of whiskey since moving to Carthage." The bartender pointed, with a glass in his hand, to the dark brown booth in the back corner of the bar. "Sometimes he sleeps it off in the booth back there."

At least we knew where Dez slept some, if not all, of the nights he didn't come home to Abby.

"He's been here for the last couple of days. Left yesterday, said he was headed home."

Dez was alive! At least he was yesterday. What could this possibly tell us? First, it could be safely assumed Dez was not on the run after killing Marco. Second, it meant whoever had killed Marco had no reason to kill someone else, at least not yet. Third, it meant Sheriff Poole was possibly the worst detective ever, since he was going to look for Dez in local bars and apparently hadn't made it to this one, because if he had, he'd have found Dez. I had to wonder, once we finally found Dez, what could he tell us about the night Marco was murdered? I hoped he hadn't pickled his brain to the point he couldn't remember any details.

Abby was going to be thrilled to hear Dez was alive. Since he hadn't shown up at home or their studio, it did make me wonder where he was now.

"Does he have some other place he likes to go? I heard there's another bar around here."

"Oh, you mean Herbie's Hideaway? Old Herb, he's been gone for a while."

"Dead?" Tessa asked.

"No, he's a taking a trip to the Caribbean. His wife's been bugging him to go for years."

"You got a ladies' room?" Tessa asked the bartender, still in her fake-drunken state.

"Sure, back there, make a left at the moose head."

Tessa jumped down from the barstool. "You coming with me?"

"No, I'm fine," I replied.

"I dunno, I might not be able to find my way," Tessa said, laying the drunken shtick on heavily.

"Right! You know us ladies, always having to go together," I said to the bartender, heading toward Tessa, the moose head looming on the wall above her.

"Is this all part of your drunken charade?" I asked Tessa.

"No, I really needed to pee," Tessa said from inside a stall. "I think we've heard all we're going to from this guy. Can we get out of here?"

"Absolutely."

After Tessa finished, we stepped into the hallway. At the other end of the bar, the front door opened, and the light from outside blasted us. It had been raining, but even with the dreary weather, it was much brighter outside than in this dimly lit bar. It was so bright we couldn't recognize who was standing in the doorway. Tessa and I crept back into the ladies' room, leaving only a crack open that we could peek through.

The bar's door swung shut as the man sat down at the bar a few seats from where our beers were.

It was Sheriff Harvey Poole.

"Crap! What do we do now?" I asked Tessa. The sheriff would be displeased to see me, and he'd want to ask me questions I simply couldn't—or wouldn't—answer. Who knew what he might do?

We looked around the dingy bathroom. I noticed Tessa eyeing the small window above the toilet in the stall.

"Oh, no, Tessa. No," I said.

"Look, you're the one who got us into trouble. Now I've got to get us out." Tessa stared at me with her fiercest take-no-prisoners glare. I knew there was no way to convince her this was a lousy plan. In fact, it appeared to be our only option, unless I wanted to trot past the sheriff and hope I could run faster than he could, which was possible.

"I give up," I said, resigned to the inevitable. After closing the toilet lid, I climbed up, pushed the window open, and peered out. It was going to be a tight fit. Fortunately, the Ladybug was below the window. If we aimed right, we should be able to land on her soft ragtop.

"Me first," Tessa said. "I'll need a boost."

"And what about me? Won't I need a boost?"

"You're much taller than I am, you'll be fine."

I stepped down from the toilet and Tessa took my place. She climbed onto the toilet tank and I stood on the seat once again, taking her heel in my hand and thrusting her headfirst out the window.

"*Che casino!*" Tessa said. I could barely hear her since her head was outside, while the rest of her dangled in the window frame a foot above me. "What do I do now? I don't want to go out this window head first. I'll break my neck."

"Hoist yourself up onto the window sill and flip yourself around," I said. Through a series of twists and turns, she finally disappeared out the window.

I climbed on top of the toilet tank as Tessa had done and looked down at her.

"Come on, your turn," Tessa said, looking up at me.

"I can't do it. I don't think I can do the origami move you did."

"I have an idea. Throw me your keys."

I rummaged through my handbag, found them, and tossed them down to her. She climbed into my car.

"Tessa! Don't you dare leave me behind," I hissed. Calmly, Tessa pushed the button for the convertible roof, and as it unhooked, its front edge slid upward toward me. She stopped the roof when it had fully extended, and its frame was within arms' reach from me.

"Grab hold!" Tessa said, trying not to shout. I boosted myself onto the sill, grabbed hold of the top edge of the convertible's roof frame, and held tight.

"Now what?" I asked.

"Now you climb down."

"I'm stuck. I can't get out the rest of the way. We've got to hurry. The bartender is probably starting to wonder what's taking us so long."

"Hang on tight. I've got this." She started driving slowly, gently pulling me from the window. Once I was freed, now clinging tightly to the hinged steel roof, Tessa stopped the car so I could climb the rest of the way down. She put the convertible's top back in place while I, finally on solid ground, took a seat on the passenger's side.

"Whew! Made it," I said.

"Let's get out of here," Tessa said, driving the Ladybug out of the far side the parking lot, staying as far away from the sheriff's patrol car as possible.

We cruised along the twisting roads toward Carthage. As Tessa sped through a curve, I spotted a set of tire tracks heading off the road.

"Stop the car," I said. Tessa pulled to the side of the road, a few feet in front of where I'd seen the tracks. As soon as the car had stopped, I was out and looking over the edge of the roadway and into the ravine below. At the bottom of the gulch was Dez's white vintage truck, the front half wrapped around the wide trunk of a fir.

"Dez!" I called down to him. "Dez!" Tessa joined me in shouting down the hill toward the truck.

"I'm going down there. You stay here so you can flag someone down if we need help," I said as I started to climb down the hill toward the truck. The slope was steep and it was slow going as I scrambled through the branches and rocks. Finally, I made it to the truck, out of breath and wet to the knees. The windows of the truck were all broken out. I peered inside. Empty.

"Dez!" I called as I searched around the vehicle. I found him near a large rock; his legs looked strange. They were pointed at an odd angle. "Oh my God, Dez!" I ran to him, falling to my knees beside him. "Dez?" His eyes were closed. I touched his face. It was warm.

"Dez, can you hear me?"

"Abby?"

"No, it's Jax. Tessa and I, we're going to take care of you. You're going to be fine. I promise." I pulled out my phone and tried to call Tessa so I wouldn't have to yell. There was no cell reception down in the ravine, so I resorted to shouting.

"Tessa!" I shouted up the hill. "I found Dez. He's alive! He needs an ambulance."

"I'm on it!" Tessa shouted back.

"Someone is coming to help you. You're going to be okay," I said, trying to sound reassuring.

"I need Abby."

"I hear you, Dez. I'll make sure Abby knows you're okay. Don't you worry."

"Thirsty," he said.

"The ambulance will be here soon and one of the EMTs will help you." I wasn't sure if he should drink anything until the extent of his injuries were known. "When help arrives, I'm going to make myself scarce because things are a little complicated for me right now." Namely, I didn't want to run into Sheriff Poole.

"You and Tessa, you're good people."

And then it hit me. He didn't know about Marco. At least I didn't think he knew. The only way he could possibly know Marco was dead was if he were the killer or if he had witnessed the murder. I hated to take advantage of an injured man, but I needed to see what I could find out from him in the few minutes I had before the ambulance, or the sheriff, arrived. This might be my only chance, especially now while his defenses were down.

"What do you think about Marco?" I asked, settling on a vague question to see where it might lead.

"He's a bastard. Always has been. I don't know why I let Abby convince me to let him come," Dez said, squeezing his eyes closed.

"Having a lot of pain?"

"Yeah, yeah, my damn legs hurt. I tried to get up and walk on them. Too much pain."

"You can wiggle your toes, right?"

"Yep, they're working, glad to say."

I didn't think I could bring up Marco again, but I didn't have to. He did.

"Hope Abby's not had too much trouble dealing with Marco without me around. I'm feeling rotten for bailing on the class. I didn't plan on being gone for so long, but then again, I didn't plan on being down here in this gulch for the last day." He didn't know about Marco. I was certain.

"Dez, I've got to tell you something. Then I've got to go because the sheriff is going to get here soon, and I really don't want to have a conversation with him right now. Okay? I don't know how to say this gently, so I'm going to come out and say it: Marco de Luca is dead. Someone murdered him, but we don't know who."

"No—how can that be?"

"I'm trying to find the killer. So, it would be great if you can tell me anything, anything at all, about what you saw on the first night of class, after everyone had gone."

"I wanted to go to this bar, but Marco said he didn't want to go. He wanted to do some work in the hot shop and then call it a night. I guess after Katia told him to go to hell, he figured he didn't have anything else to do. Crap, I guess he should have come out with me; maybe he'd be alive today if he had. Of course, he might have ended up down in this ravine with a couple of broken legs, but it beats the hell out of being dead." That was for sure.

Voices floated down from the road above us. That was my cue to get out of there.

"Someone will be down to help you in a few minutes. I've got to go. I'm sorry."

I scrambled up the hill, breaking out of the bushes near the Ladybug's front bumper. I had a stitch in my side from climbing up the hill and found myself, once again covered in mud. Tessa was talking with the EMT, who was pulling his gear out of the back of the ambulance. There was no sign of the sheriff. I slid into the passenger seat of my car, breathing hard, and waited for her. Moments later, Tessa pulled herself into the Ladybug, and we took off. She drove at a more reasonable speed, after having seen what happened to Dez on this curving, dangerous road. I dialed Zachary.

"It's Jax," I said when he answered.

"I didn't even need to look at caller ID. I knew it was going to be you. Don't tell me you're in trouble already."

"Well..."

Zachary sighed. It was not a happy sigh, and it was very loud.

"What is it?"

"We found Dez."

"And was he alive and well and drunk out of his mind?"

"Alive, but pretty banged up. He's been at the bottom of a ravine for the last day. His legs are broken, I'm pretty sure, but I think he's going to live."

"If you are anywhere near Dez, I suggest you get out of there. If the sheriff shows up, things could get messy," Zachary said.

"An ambulance arrived, so Tessa and I have already left."

"Where'd you find him?"

"He's down in a gulch about a half mile from The Office."

"Whose office?"

"It's a bar. If you're coming out this way and happen to go by there, can you do me a favor? Can you leave them ten bucks for a couple of drinks? We had to escape before paying for them."

"Escape?"

"I'm pretty sure you don't want to hear about it."

He sighed again. "I'm pretty sure you're right."

TWENTY-THREE

TESSA DROVE US BACK to Old Firehouse Studio.

We found Abby pacing her office, looking as haggard as I'd ever seen her.

"Abby! We found Dez," Tessa said. "And he's alive, a little banged up, though."

"Thank God!" Abby collapsed into Tessa's arms and hugged her. "Where was he? What happened?"

"We found him in a ravine a few miles from here. It looks like he drove off the road, probably because of the rain. He wrapped his truck around a tree," Tessa said.

"Is he okay?"

"He's on his way to the hospital. It looks like he has a couple of broken legs and is pretty dehydrated, but he's going to survive," I said. "He kept asking for you."

"Oh, thank you so much for finding him," Abby said, her voice catching in her throat. "You know, he may be a stubborn jerk, but he's my stubborn jerk. I better figure out where they're taking him." Abby picked up the phone, ready to dial. "Thank you, both, for everything."

I stepped into the hot shop to announce to the class that Dez had been found alive. Dario was alone, working on his laptop. The students were cutting and grinding their canes with Sam in the utility yard.

"*Ciao*, Jax. Nice of you to stop by. You haven't abandoned glassblowing, have you?"

"No, I needed to help Abby out. And guess what? We found Dez!"

"That's great news. Did you learn anything from him? Does he know who killed my brother? Did he confess to killing Marco?"

"I'm afraid none of the above. He didn't know Marco was dead. Dez was in bad shape. He was banged up after careening into a ravine and crashing his truck, so I don't think he had much capacity to lie."

"I understand. So, Dez is not Marco's killer."

"I don't think so," I said. "And what about you? What sleuthing have you been able to do? Has anyone been acting strange?"

"I'm afraid I'm a rotten detective. I haven't been able to find out much of anything. Everyone in class seems pleased, everyone except Violetta."

"Have you seen any of the beads Violetta is selling?"

"Sure, of course. I even recognize some of them. They came from my nonna's house."

Tessa entered the hot shop, catching the last few words of our conversation.

"Your nonna's house? Beads like these?" Tessa asked, pulling the beads she'd filched from Violetta from her purse and handing them to Dario.

"Oh, ha! Yes, like these. You know, we have this funny thing we liked to say about these beads."

"That they came from your grandmother's basement?" Tessa asked.

"How'd you know?" he asked.

"Violetta told me."

"My nonna's palazzo on the *Fondamenta Nuova* had been sinking for years. She finally decided to install some new pillars underneath it before the whole thing fell into the Venetian lagoon. She hired some divers to put a new support system in place. While they were under her house, they found a cache of beads. No one had ever seen anything like them. Who knows how long they'd been under there? A lot of them were prototypes, tossed in the canal because at the time they were rejected. The designs were too strange, a lot of them were purple. No one wanted that funereal color back in the old days. When the divers brought them up from the depths, we joked that they were from my nonna's basement."

"Violetta must not have known it was a joke. So these beads are the real thing?" I asked.

"Absolutely. And it's sad, because these beads are worth a lot more than Violetta is selling them for."

"I guess we're not rich and famous enough to afford them," Tessa said, without a hint of meanness in her voice.

"Speaking of rich and famous, if you are trying to draw out the killer, you might want to try to act a little more like Marco did. Maybe a little more swagger? Whatever Marco did, that's what set off the killer. Maybe you're being a little too nice."

"Are you saying my brother wasn't nice?"

"No. It's that he was, uh, was a little more, cocky, I mean, I'm sorry—"

"I get it. He was always more confident than me, always better at being a showman. I'll see what I can do to channel my inner Marco."

The students returned to the studio, each holding trays of their newly cut murrine. All except Duke, who was noticeably absent.

Dario inspected the students' murrine and praised their work. Everyone had done a first-rate job making canes, and I could tell Dario was proud of what the students had done with his guidance.

"Now, Jax, you still have not made a cane. Can we try again?" Dario asked.

"Well, I..."

"Come on, Jax, you can do it," Tessa said.

"Okay. Fine! I'll do it." I grabbed a punty with both hands and marched to the furnace, determined to gather some glass. I mean, really, how hard could it be? Everyone else in the class had done it, even the Twins, who were now watching me from the sidelines. Dario opened the furnace door a crack and I slid the punty in. I stood back and tried to see into the molten inferno in front of me. I had no idea if I'd touched the glass in the crucible with my punty or not. I yanked it out of the furnace. A pencil-thin drizzle of glass came out with the punty. It was pathetic.

Sara and Lara tried to contain their laughter.

"Looks like you'll have to keep using the murrine we left for you at Tessa's studio," one of them said.

"Pretty funny," the other said with a snicker.

"What? You two are the ones who are leaving me murrine with death threats!"

"It was only a joke," said the first one.

"We thought you'd be into it. You're always so interested in murder," said the other.

"What am I supposed to do with this glass?" I asked Dario, choosing to ignore the Twins. I'd have to deal with them later, but for now I was relieved to know it hadn't been a real death threat.

"Put it in the crack-off bucket there at your feet," Dario said.

With a little too much gusto, I pushed the punty into the water and listened to the satisfying *pish* sound as the hot glass crackled into a million pieces when it hit the cold water. Looking into the crack-off bucket, I could see the tiny bits of clear glass gravel from my pathetic gather. I removed the punty, now free of glass, and set it aside. I left the hot shop, still a failure, and went in search of coffee.

When I entered the kitchen, Tessa was saying good-bye to Violetta, who was packing her beads and getting ready to go. I expected Tessa would find a convenient way of slipping the beads she'd "borrowed" back into Violetta's inventory. At this point, Violetta could officially be removed from the list of suspects now that Dario confirmed the silly truth about Marco and Dario's grandmother. She was the only woman in Venice with a basement full of beads.

Someone had placed an *out of order* sign on the Mr. Coffee in the kitchen. It was definitely time for me to head to the Robin's Nest Café.

TWENTY-FOUR

I RECEIVED A CALL from my sister as I walked to the café.

"I've got some news for you about the de Luca brothers' estate," Connie said.

"What did you find out?"

"It looks like the fancy property where Dario lives isn't owned by the family, it's leased. So, there isn't much the brothers were going to share, and it doesn't seem to me one of them would kill the other for both shares. Of course, there may be more property in Italy that might be worth committing fratricide for, but I don't have access to that kind of international information."

It didn't seem likely Dario was Marco's killer. I was relieved to know we could check him off our list of suspects.

"Thanks. That's really helpful information. We haven't found our killer, but at least you've helped me narrow it down a little bit more."

"Gotta run, Jax, talk with you again soon," Connie said.

I pushed open the door to the café. Carl was standing in his usual spot.

"Hello there! Flying solo, I see. Want to sit at the counter?"

"Sure. A cup of coffee, please," I said, taking a seat. "What kind of muffins do you have today?"

"Sorry, I'm afraid Vickie's not here. No Vickie means no muffins. She's visiting our daughter."

"Is that a picture of her by the front door?" I considered playing dumb and asking about what had happened to his daughter, but instead I cut to the chase. "She was hit by a car, right?"

"That's right. What, was Dez bragging about how he mowed our daughter down? Is that how you found out?"

"No, of course not. I read about it somewhere." I decided to skip the part about how my cyber-sleuth brother had filled me in on the details of Carl's lawsuit against Abby and Dez. "It must have been horrible for you and your family."

"Must have been? You're talking as if what happened from this accident is in the past. We're living with this every day. Robin is still in rehab, still needs more surgery, and is all the way down in Tacoma. Vickie tries to get over to her as often as she can, but that's hard to do."

"I'm sorry. I didn't realize your daughter hadn't fully recovered."

"I'm not sure she, or any of us, will ever recover entirely. We're trying to sell this café so we can move to Tacoma and be a little closer to Robin in the rehab facility, but the only offers we've gotten have been low-ball—a pittance." Carl's bright smile faded. He picked up a rag and started feverishly wiping down the counter. "And we still have Dez out there driving his car around like a maniac, drunk as usual."

"Are you certain it was him?"

"Of course, it was him. It had to be him. Robin said it was a man in a light-colored pickup truck," Carl said, chucking the rag into a bucket on the floor. "Then we tried to sue them, you know? Tried to get some money out of them so we could get out of this depressing place, away from our terrible memories. I mean, she nearly bled to death on the street outside this window. But we lost the suit. We couldn't prove it was him, but I know it was."

I thought of Dez, who at this moment was at the hospital, his own legs damaged from his reckless driving.

"Oh, Carl, I'm so very sorry. I wish there was something I

could do."

"Do you know anyone who wants to buy a café in the middle of nowhere?"

"I don't. But I'd love a refill on my coffee." I slid the cup over to him.

"You got it."

Glancing out the window, I saw the tow truck pulling Dez's vintage pickup into the garage across the street. Tony Stein, the automotive genius who got the Ladybug back in working order, had recovered Dez's pickup. I wanted to have a talk with him. I slugged down the rest of my coffee and left five dollars on the counter for Carl, who had disappeared into the back, most likely to regroup after his emotional outburst.

I crossed Main Street, a chill running down my spine as I thought about Robin Nest being struck in the road, her crumpled body left behind while the driver of a pickup truck, Dez's or someone else's, didn't bother to stop after hitting the poor girl.

"Knock, knock! Hey, Tony, I brought the bead you wanted for your sister," I said, coming into the garage and leaving the bead on the counter by the cash register.

Tony was busy looking under the front end of Dez's pickup.

"Oh, hey, Jax," Tony said, lost in thought.

"What's up? Is there something wrong with Dez's car, other than the obvious?" I asked, noting that the entire bumper and half the hood had been caved in by the tree Dez hit in the ravine.

"As a matter of fact, there is. Check this out," Tony said, pulling on a cable that was hanging loose under the truck. You know what these are?"

"No."

"Brake lines. And see these slices in the sheathing right here? Somebody cut the brake lines on Dez's pickup."

TWENTY-FIVE

"COULD THE BRAKE LINES have been like this for a while?" I asked Tony.

"Oh, I don't think so. This was no accident. It's not wear and tear on the brake lines. Someone caused this damage on purpose."

"Have you ever done any repair on Dez's truck before?"

"No, I don't recall ever fixing it."

"How about someone else's pickup, say, around six to nine months ago. Maybe you repaired a bumper?" I wondered if whoever had hit Robin Nest last summer would have damaged their car. If they hit her hard enough to injure her severely, I would have thought so. I'd expect the culprit would want to repair their car quickly and quietly to avoid having to answer any questions about how their vehicle had been damaged.

"You know nearly everyone in this area has a pickup truck, right?"

"I hadn't thought about that. I guess you're saying there are a lot of truck bumpers out there that you've replaced in the last several months."

"Yeah, I guess I need to sell them to the scrap dealer soon," Tony said, nodding to the junk yard behind his garage.

"Can I take a look at them?" I wasn't sure what I was looking for, but wondered if one of these bumpers might hold a clue to help find the person who hit Robin Nest. Tony took me out back.

"Most of these have been around less than a year. This one's from a pick-up, and so are these two." He pulled out the bumpers from the pile and laid them on the ground.

"None of these is from a vintage pickup truck like Dez had, right?"

"No, I don't get too many of those. This one is from a Toyota. Looks like whoever it was hit a tree, judging from the scrape marks. Yeah. I remember this guy."

"What about this one?" I asked, setting the first bumper aside and pointing at another one.

"Oh, this one, he rear ended a red sports car. See the red paint?"

"And what about this one?"

"Yeah, he hit a deer. You can still a little dried blood on it."

"Do you remember whose truck this was?"

"I'd have to look back in my records. You want me to do that?"

"Yes, please. And don't get rid of that bumper. Somehow, I think it might help Dez."

"Poor guy, you know he was accused of hurting that girl across the street at the café?"

"What do you know about that?"

"Not much. But he's been doing some snooping around, trying to figure out who ran over her. He's been looking at some of my security camera footage from that day."

"Dez was trying to find out who hit Robin?"

"Yeah, I think so, but I'm worried he may have done something rash, pissed off someone enough that they wanted him dead. Why else would his brake lines have been cut?"

• • •

I walked back to the studio to pick up Tessa. The other students had left for the day, and Tessa was chatting with Dario in Italian. They switched to English as I approached.

"Have fun blowing glass tonight," Tessa said. "*Ciao.*"

"*Ciao, ciao,*" Dario replied.

As we drove back toward Seattle for the umpteenth time that week, I told Tessa what I'd learned from Carl and Tony.

"Who would want to cut Dez's brake lines?" Tessa asked.

"That's an easy answer. Carl! He was crystal clear about how much he blames Dez for nearly killing his daughter. He even sued him. When that failed, it looks like he took matters into his own hands."

"But if Dez was trying to find the person who hit Robin, if we assume it wasn't him, then perhaps Dez spooked the real culprit. Now that person is trying to silence him," Tessa said.

"That's a pretty good motive, but who would that be?"

"I don't know. It's probably not Abby. She seemed genuinely troubled by Dez's disappearance."

"Other people might have a reason to kill Marco, right?"

"Right. I mean, really it could be any one of us."

"But not either one of us."

"But anyone at Old Firehouse Studio."

"Sure, but you know, almost anyone who was sufficiently motivated could have come to the studio that night, if they'd known Marco was there."

"And had a reason to want him dead."

•   •   •

I dropped Tessa off at my house so she could get her car and drive to Fremont Fire to take care of a few business matters. Now I could do some sleuthing on my own.

Duke's glassblowing studio was tucked in the center of an industrial pocket of streets south of Seattle's downtown. I found the entrance and dashed through the rain, nearly running into a young man carrying a tub filled with water and glass shards. Inside the studio, Duke was shouting at him.

"Idiot! How many times do I need to tell you? You've got to keep the colored glass out of the crack-off bucket. I can only recycle the clear—" Duke saw me and stopped in mid-sentence. "What are you doing here? Oh, I get it. Abby sent you to get me to come to class."

"No. I came on my own."

"I already explained to Abby, unless Marco is back from the dead, I'm not returning to Old Firehouse Studio."

"Not even if his brother were teaching class?"

"Yeah, Abby called me and told me about Dario, but seriously? He hasn't blown glass in years, there's no way Abby would be able to convince him."

"Abby didn't have to. Tessa did."

"Huh. I don't know…It would be good to see Dario."

"You know Dario?" The glass world was small, so it wasn't surprising that the men knew each other, but somehow, I thought I would have known that by now. "You knew Marco?"

"Oh, sure, I've known both of them for years. Can't say I've been in touch with them much." I recalled the first night of class when Marco was rude to Duke. At the time I thought it was Marco reacting to Duke's surly attitude. In fact, there was some personal history there and that had most likely intensified Marco's reaction to him. Duke brought me over to a wall of photos at the back of his workshop. "Let me show you something. Here we are at Hillside Studios in Montana. None of us had slept for days. We were partying and blowing glass. It was our last night, and, oh, we were going to have a massive hangover the next day," Duke chuckled, the first sign of humor I'd ever seen in the man.

I gazed at the photo. A group of ten men and one woman stood with their arms around each other, smiling, each holding a blowpipe. I focused more closely on the woman.

"Is that Abby?"

"As a matter of fact, it is. She and I go way back."

"And Dez, too?"

"Oh yeah, he was there, messed up with the rest of us. And there's Marco and Dario, right in the middle."

Off to the side, nearly out of the frame, one man caught my eye. Who was that guy? The one wearing the *Ciao* T-shirt with the burn mark on the left sleeve.

TWENTY-SIX

I HEADED TO THE HOMICIDE DIVISION offices of the Seattle P.D.

I'd visited Zachary's office last year when he demanded that Tessa and I show up so he could question us about the murder of a young woman whose body we discovered behind Aztec Beads. Zachary had been quite stern with me back then, though he certainly had warmed up in recent months. In thinking it through, now that I was walking down the hall toward his office, I probably should have called to ask if I could come by. Realizing I should not have come unannounced, I decided a quick retreat was the best course of action and made a spontaneous U-turn, smacking right into none other than Zachary himself.

"You came by my office, how nice," Zachary said. "I hope this is a social visit."

"I brought you your handkerchief," I said, pulling it out of my handbag and handing it to him.

"You certainly didn't come all this way to give me that." Dammit. He saw right through me.

"Um, yes, well, also," I said, flustered, because I was weighing my options. Should I tell him the truth, that I was there on a mission to find Marco de Luca's killer? Or should I fib and tell him I had come only to see him? I didn't need to answer. Zachary figured it out on his own. He was a detective, after all.

"I see. So maybe I was too hopeful that you'd want to stop by and see me? And maybe too hopeful, as well, that you'd leave this murder investigation alone?"

"You need to hear me out, okay? I have an idea, and I don't think it's too crazy." Zachary grasped my elbow and ushered me toward his office. I wriggled out of his grip. "Please. I'm sorry to be meddling, but I think I've got something here. I need to see the Medical Examiner. Actually, I need to see Marco."

"Marco? Trust me, Jax, you do not want to see a body after it's been through an autopsy. It's not a pretty sight." Zachary pulled off his heavy-rimmed glasses and rubbed his eyes. For the brief moment while his glasses were off, I remembered how incredibly sexy he was, and longed to spend some time with him, and not at the police department. Zachary put his glasses back on, and I snapped out of my reverie, which was a good thing since I was getting a little carried away thinking about what we could do together.

"Actually, I need to see his T-shirt, the one he was found dead in."

"You don't need to see Marco's body to see that shirt. It's in evidence. What do you think it will tell us?"

"I'm not sure, but I don't think it was his shirt."

"Certainly, someone wouldn't commit murder because Marco stole his shirt," Zachary said in a dismissive tone.

"I want to see if the shirt I saw in a picture at a local glassblower's workshop is the same one Marco had on the night he died. It has the word *Ciao* in fancy script across the front of it."

"Certainly, there could be more than one T-shirt like that," Zachary said.

He dropped me off in his office and went to pull the shirt from the evidence center. While he was gone, I sent a text to Vance asking him to send me one of the pictures he took from the first night of class, hoping it would reveal another clue that would lead us to the killer. I removed a stack of files from Zachary's only guest chair and sat down. When he returned, he pulled the T-shirt out of a plastic evidence bag and spread it out a metal tray.

"What are we looking for?" Zachary asked.

"We're looking at the holes."

"The holes?"

"See, there's one here on the left sleeve. I saw someone wearing a shirt like this in a picture from ten years ago. Back then it was a burn mark, and now it's a hole."

"There are all sorts of holes in this shirt," Zachary said. "Let's see what the M.E. has to say in her report," Zachary said, pulling up the report on his computer screen and reading aloud. "'Subject exposed for thirty-plus hours...' sounds like he was pretty bloated by the time she did the autopsy. The M.E. said there was low blood loss at the point of entry of the weapon, indicative of what, she was not certain."

"But he was dead before he went in the river, right? Tessa did see Marco in the hot shop and he was already dead."

"Yes, right here it says there was water in his airway, but not in his lungs. He didn't drown," Zachary said, pointing at the computer screen.

"She doesn't say anything about the shirt?"

"No, but she's a medical examiner, not a detective. She cares about what the body can tell her."

"So, who's the detective working on this case? Is it you?" I asked.

"I'm working to get this case transferred to me, but so far your buddy Sheriff Poole isn't letting go of it, so I can only work on this in an unofficial capacity. But, I've got to say, looking at this shirt, all I see is a shirt with burn holes in it. I don't see a cut from a knife."

My phone pinged. It was a message from Vance, with the photo I'd hoped he would send. I zoomed in on the picture of Marco's shirt. I showed Zachary the picture on my phone that Vance had taken the night Marco had died with all of the students gathered around him in Old Firehouse Studio's kitchen. Marco was wearing his holey *Ciao* shirt, only there was one less hole in it than there was in the shirt on the desk in front of us.

"This burn hole right here," I said, pointing to the hole in the center of the *o* in *Ciao* on the T-shirt. "There was no hole there the last time we saw Marco alive."

"And what does that tell us?" Zachary asked, taking off his glasses to look more closely at the hole in the center of the *o*.

"What does the M.E.'s report say about glass? Did she find any glass in the wound in Marco's chest?"

Zachary tapped the keys on his keyboard. "Hm. Doesn't say she found anything."

"How hard would it be for her to look again?"

"I can make the request. Why?"

"Because I think I know what the murder weapon is," I said.

"We had a CSI team out there all day scouring Carthage, the studio, the river, Main Street. We didn't find a weapon that matched the wound. Your knife doesn't match it, you'll be pleased to know."

"They're not going to find it. If you come over tonight, I can show you."

TWENTY-SEVEN

I ANSWERED THE DOOR at seven o'clock. There was only one problem. The man standing on my welcome mat was not Zachary, but Ryan.

"Ryan? What the heck are you doing here?"

He shoved a bouquet of purple tulips at me.

"These are for you. Please, accept my apology for pulling Tessa over, and uh, pulling her over again."

"And for rescuing me from the clutches of Sheriff Poole," I added.

"Okay, except I'm not sorry about that. I'm glad I was able to help you."

"But didn't you get into a lot of trouble?"

"I did," admitted Ryan. "But I'm sure it will be fine."

Gumdrop met us on the landing by the front door, and I picked him up. I had an idea. I stepped onto the porch and knocked on Val's door.

"I won't be but a second."

Val opened the door a crack.

"Can you do me a favor? Gummie needs to be groomed, right now. It's urgent."

"What? Grooming? I didn't say I'd groom him. I'm a hairdresser for humans, not pets. Although I did give Stanley a bath after his romp in the mud with you." Val looked at me like I was a crazy person. What I needed was for Val to rescue me by getting rid of Ryan. She needed to do it fast, because Zachary would be here soon and I didn't want to see those two clash.

"Oh, I thought you said when Ryan arrives I should bring you Gumdrop." I glared at her, hoping she'd catch my drift. She had no idea what was going on. "You know, you should really say hello to Ryan, maybe invite him over to um…"

Freddie sauntered up behind Val.

"What a beautiful looking animal you've got there. I'd be happy to take him for a little while. And Valerie, it seems like maybe you should invite that nice young man in, too," Uncle Freddie said, pulling Ryan inside and grabbing Gumdrop as well.

One thing was certain, while Val was clueless about what I was trying to do, Uncle Freddie had it all figured out. For now, at least, Ryan was out of the way.

When Zachary arrived, I took him back to my studio. I showed him some of my beads, the glass-working and jewelry-making tools, the dozens of colors of Italian glass rods I stored upright in mugs and vases, and my table-mounted torch.

"My torch runs on oxygen and natural gas, and I light it like this," I said, using a striker to create a spark, while the gas flowed from the tip of the torch. The gases ignited, and soon I had the perfect eight-inch long blue flame, hot enough to melt glass. This was my comfort zone, when it came to melting glass. It was certainly much more manageable for me than the incredibly hot furnace that I simply couldn't seem to master.

"I had no idea how this all worked," he said, as I introduced a long thin rod of glass into the flame and heated it until it glowed orange. As the glass melted, it balled up at the end of the rod. I pulled it out of the flame and using my tweezers I pinched the molten blob of glass and pulled it out to a thin, needle-sharp point.

"See this? Imagine if it were eight inches long instead of an inch? Marco was stabbed with a glass knife. And the glass must have been hot when Marco was stabbed. That's why there's a burn hole, and not a cut, in his shirt."

"I could see that, but where is the weapon? Officers have searched the studio and surrounding area, and can't find anything that matches the wound."

I plunged the still-hot glass needle into an old mug of water on my workbench, my miniature version of the hot shop's crack-off bucket. The glass instantly broke into a million pieces in the bottom of the cup.

"The disappearing weapon. How ingenious," Zachary said.

"That's why I wanted to see if the M.E. had found any glass in Marco's wound. I was wondering if maybe some pieces would have chipped off if they struck a bone when he was stabbed."

"Let me check and see if there have been any updates to the files from the M.E. after my inquiry about glass in the victim's wound. Can I borrow your laptop?" Zachary asked.

I grabbed my computer and we settled down on the sofa. Zachary logged in to the police department system, jumping though all the security hoops to get to the appropriate screen, which showed him the updates from the Medical Examiner.

"Aha! It looks like the M.E. found three small pieces of glass, each two millimeters wide," Zachary said.

"So, I'd say that confirms it. The murder weapon was a glass knife. I haven't had enough courage to blow glass at all, so I'm not in the running as the murderer. I couldn't make a glass knife even if I had wanted to kill Marco."

"I'm pleased to hear that," Zachary said. "I wouldn't want to have to arrest you." He gave me a gentle kiss on the lips. "I wouldn't want to throw you in jail," he added with another kiss, this one a little more intense than the last.

I was getting pretty hot and bothered.

"What else would you *not* want to do?" I asked, teasing him.

"I definitely would want to put you in handcuffs," he said with a sly smile.

"What? You *would* or *wouldn't* want to put me in handcuffs?"

Zachary was flustered now, as he clearly had slipped up and not said exactly what he meant. Or had he?"

"A-hem!" He cleared his throat and tried again. "You know, I wouldn't want to do anything—uh, that would—uh, put you in a compromising position, I mean, uh, complicated, or uncomfortable position."

"Shhhh," I said, giving him a kiss. "I think it's better if we don't use our words right now.

• • •

As we stood on the front porch, Zachary kissed me one last time. I felt a tingle all the way down to my toes. Since Tessa was staying with me, we couldn't have gotten any more serious than kissing for fear that she might come home and catch us in a compromising position, to use Zachary's slip of the tongue.

Zachary turned and trotted down the front steps and waved as he got inside his car. I sighed. Even though he was serious and at times awkward, he had a gentleness that attracted me. I was definitely starting to have feelings for this complicated man.

I tapped on Val's front door, hopeful that Ryan had already left and that I wouldn't have to deal with him again tonight.

Val peeked out at me.

"What do you want?" she asked.

"Is Ryan still with you?"

"No. Come in," Val said opening the door far enough to allow me to slide inside. "So, did you have a nice time with Zachary?"

I decided to try the strategy Tessa used to avoid answering questions.

"It's complicated."

"Come on. Did you have a really, really nice time?"

"It's very complicated."

"I don't think she's ready to talk about it." Uncle Freddie was sitting on the sofa strumming an acoustic guitar. "She doesn't want to 'Kiss and Tell'," he said, playing a riff from that Bryan Ferry song. Freddie was definitely more tuned into what was going on with other people than Val, and I liked that about him.

"I thought you came to tell me about how you finally pointed your heels up to heaven, if you get my drift," Val said with wink.

"Sorry, my heels were firmly on the ground. I just came to retrieve Gumdrop."

"Oh, right! Let me go get him." Val headed down the hall, returned with my cat in her arms, and passed him to me. "Gumdrop sure seemed to like Ryan—what a hunk!"

I hefted Gumdrop in my arms. "I don't know, Gummie, you seem pretty hunky to me—or maybe that's chunky? As for Ryan, he does have a lot of animal magnetism, but I'm afraid that may be his only asset. Thanks for taking care of Gummie and Ryan," I said, making a quick escape so Val couldn't continue to grill me about how I'd spent the evening.

Returning to my studio, I shut off the oxygen and natural gas to my torch. Gumdrop jumped onto my workbench and cruised over to see what I was doing. I gave him a long stroke down his back, and he closed his big green eyes and began to purr. He flopped onto his side, pushing the mug of water over. Water and bits of glass gravel rushed across the table top. As soon as the water hit Gumdrop's paws, he leapt from the table, and was gone.

"Dammit, Gummie," I said, grabbing some paper towels to sop up the liquid. I used a little whisk broom to sweep up the bits of glass. As I looked at the bits of glass, I was struck with a memory. I remembered seeing colored glass in the hot-shop's crack-off bucket the first time I worked with Dario in the studio. But, the last time I worked with him the bucket was clean, except for the small bit of clear glass that I had deposited when I'd placed my tiny gather of glass into it. If the colored glass in the crack-off bucket was from the murder weapon, then that could tell us who the culprit was. I wished I could remember what color it was, but I just couldn't recall.

I called Tessa.

"Are you still at your studio?"

"Why? Do you and Zachary need a little more time?"

"What? No. He just left."

"Oh! Ha! That was only a guess—he was actually there? And how was the stern detective?"

"Not that stern, more like stumbling. Every once in a while, he says something completely wrong and embarrassing—sort of like a Freudian slip. It's like he's repressed, and occasionally something inappropriate pops out. Anyway, I sent him home a little while ago."

I filled Tessa in on my idea that Marco had been killed with a glass knife and that the knife had been destroyed by being thrown in the crack-off bucket and shattered.

"Jax, you are a genius," Tessa said. "What does Zachary think of your theory?"

"He thought it was brilliant. He said the killer's weapon was ingenious, actually."

"Well, it is."

"But there's one problem. Just knowing Marco was killed with a glass knife doesn't point us to the killer. The M.E. missed the glass the first time she autopsied Marco. That tells me she had a hard time seeing the glass. It could have been clear—everyone had access to the clear glass," I said. "Which doesn't help us narrow down the list of suspects. I saw colored glass in the crack off bucket, but I just can't recall what color it was."

"I've got samples of everyone's murrine right here. I was going to make a display of them for my shop. Maybe this will jog your memory," Tessa said. "Okay…Vance's murrine are orange. Duke's are green. Lara's and Sara's are black and ivory. Katia's murrine are purple. And here's my sample. It's blue."

"Seems like any of those colors would have been easy for the medical examiner to locate in Marco's body, and it doesn't help me recall the color. All I know is that it's a big no-no to put colored glass in the crack-off bucket. I even heard Duke yelling at his assistant about it. That doesn't get us anywhere," I said.

"I'm leaving my shop now and will see you in a few minutes. Why don't you settle down and I'll be there soon."

I poured myself a glass of milk, and decided one of Val's chocolate cupcakes would be a good accompaniment. I settled onto my sofa. A message popped up on my laptop, which was sitting on the coffee table. To my surprise it was still logged in to the Seattle P.D. page that Zachary and I had been looking at before we had moved on to more interesting activities.

Session expiring in five minutes. Press Okay to stay logged in or press Logout to end this session.

I took a bite of cupcake and pressed *Okay*. Then I read the autopsy report. I scrolled to the bottom of the report, skipping such gruesome details as the weight of Marco's liver. I wanted to read about the glass that was found in the wound. And there it was.

Three fragments of glass two millimeters wide.

Then I noticed something. A little paper clip icon. There was an image associated with this note. I clicked on it and a photo appeared: three tiny pieces of glass. Pink glass.

Tessa walked in the back door and headed to the living room. I quickly closed the lid of my laptop. She would most likely not approve of my logging into Zachary's account without him present. Tessa turned the corner into the living room while I sat on the couch trying to look nonchalant, and took another bite of my cupcake.

"You look like you are up to no good," she said.

"I'll never admit it, even if I am. But get this, and don't ask how I know: The glass in Marco's wound was pink. That's why the M.E. missed it the first time she looked."

"Pink glass! Don't you remember about the pink glass powder Dez had out the night Marco died?"

"Right! He kept it locked up because it was expensive."

If the glass knife had been made of pink glass, then there were exactly three people who had access to that glass: Abby, Dez, and Sam.

Sam. It had to be him. But why?

"Tessa? Did I hear you talking with Dario about blowing glass tonight?"

"Yes—oh no! If Sam killed Marco, and Dario is out there alone with Sam right now, then—"

"He could be in danger," I said.

"You better call the sheriff."

I dialed the sheriff's number with shaky hands.

"Sheriff Poole? It's Jax O'Connell," I said when he answered, squeezing my eyes tight and waiting for his tirade.

"Well, well, well. You've got some new plan to hoodwink me? Why don't you 'fess up and tell me what you've got cooking, because I'm not in the mood to play any more games with you, Ms. O'Connell."

"I'm not calling to play any games. And just so you know, I didn't have anything to do with what Ryan Shaw did the day he took me away."

"You certainly did benefit from his shenanigans, didn't ya? The main thing is, you never trusted me to do a decent job on the investigation. You came out here and acted like you were smarter than me. And you know what—"

"Excuse me, Sheriff Poole? I'm sorry to interrupt, but I think something terrible is about to happen—or may have already happened—at the glassblowing studio. I believe the instructor is in danger, the new instructor, that is."

"Right. And I'm supposed to go out there and see what's happening, all because you've got some paranoid idea about the scary things that can happen out here in the sticks."

"There was a murder, so I'm not paranoid. Do you suppose—"

"I could rush over to Old Firehouse Studio? Maybe I will, but not because you've got some far-fetched idea in your fluffy little head. But I will tell you this: If I find you trying to be a hero, I will arrest you for obstruction of justice —and your little friend, too!" He hung up.

I grabbed my purse and headed out the door.

"We're going to Carthage?" Tessa asked.

"We just need to make sure Dario is safe. We don't have to be heroes, let's just get him out of the hot shop."

And I hoped we didn't get caught by the sheriff…or the murderer.

TWENTY-EIGHT

WE TROMPED ALONG THE RIVER'S EDGE toward Old Firehouse Studio. I'd parked the Ladybug a few hundred yards away so my car wouldn't arouse the suspicions of anyone working in the hot shop or the sheriff, if he happened to drive by. It was unusually dark. The stars were obscured by the cloudy sky—a sign that more rain was imminent. We crept up the slope into the utility yard behind the building, trying to keep low, behind the bushes. Peeking in the back windows, we spotted someone moving through the studio, illuminated only by the light of the furnace.

As we turned the corner, the door opened, and Sam confronted us.

"Hello there," he said with a smile that made my skin crawl.

"Uh, hi, Sam," I said, trying to act casual while crouched on the ground. Sam yanked me up to a standing position.

I brushed myself off. "I lost my keys around here somewhere," I said, looking on the ground. "Tessa, do you see my car keys?"

Sam pulled my purse out of my hands and rummaged around inside, ready to prove me wrong. He removed his hand from my purse, a key ring with a purple handmade glass bead dangling from his index finger. "You mean these?"

"Oh, great. Thanks. My purse is so messy; I didn't realize they were in there. I guess I need to be going." I tried to grab my handbag from Sam. He didn't let go.

"Come on, Sam, give me my purse."

He threw my keys into the field.

"No, I don't think I'll do that. In fact, I'd like you to come along with me." Sam grabbed my forearm. Tessa turned to run, stumbled, and hit the ground. He caught her by the wrist and pulled her up forcefully, then pushed us into the hot shop, locking the door behind him.

"First, let's get rid of that phone. It's too tempting." Sam opened the furnace door and chucked my phone in. I watched helplessly as it melted into the molten lava before he closed the door and turned back to me.

"Where's Dario?" Tessa asked.

"He's down at the motel. He said he needed to take care of some personal business, but I think he may turn out to be as much of a womanizer as his brother. He's off with Katia, I bet," Sam said. "Marco wanted her, and you know what? He couldn't have her, because she belonged to me." I wondered if Sam and Katia had ever had a relationship—other than teacher and student—or if that was just wishful thinking on Sam's part.

I was relieved to hear Dario was out of danger, and I wished we could say the same for ourselves.

"People don't really belong to other people. You know that, right? Now, let us go, we haven't done anything wrong," Tessa said.

"Wrong? You've been wrong all along—you, Marco, Dario, and Violetta—you stuck-up Italians. You come in here acting like you own the place—so important. So much better than everyone else." Sam grabbed Tessa and pushed her backward onto the glassblower's bench. She cracked her head on the corner of the bench and hit the floor. She was out cold.

Sam turned to me. "And you, you've had a difficult time this week, frightened of this big pot of molten glass. How pathetic. I think you're going to have a tragic glassblowing accident, since you're unaccustomed to being in a studio where real glass artists work. That would be such a shame. Then again, it would be a bigger shame if you went blabbing to everyone that I'd done something wrong.

"Have you done something wrong?" I asked, trying to sound calm and backing away from him as he pressed toward me.

"Me? No. I think I may have made the world a little better place. And now, you—I'm going to make you a better person. Why don't I teach you a lesson? You're going to get a gather of glass from the furnace." Sam thrust a punty into my hands and opened the door to the furnace. The heat blasted me, more intensely than I'd ever felt.

"Get yourself some glass," he said, grabbing me by the back of the neck. Squinting against the heat, I pushed the punty into the furnace and then pulled it out quickly. A fist-sized blob of glass hung from the end of the punty. Sam slammed the furnace door shut and dragged me to the tool bench. He grabbed a pair of over-sized tweezers and pulled the now-cooling glass into a sharp point while I stood there, too terrified to drop the punty, helpless. There was no escape. The rolling door was padlocked, and I knew I couldn't overpower Sam. Even if I could escape, I would never leave Tessa behind.

"Now, look at this remarkable point. You know what's so lovely about it? You can go right over to a person, and plunge a glass knife through their chest, and they die. Bam! They're dead. And it's so clean, there's no blood, because the heat cauterizes the flesh as you stab right into a body. It worked really well on Marco, that pompous—"

"Come on, Sam. Let us go. We didn't have anything to do with what you thought of Marco."

"You know, he didn't even remember me from Hillside Studios. No, I was only the lowly punty boy. I gave him my T-shirt, literally gave him the shirt off my back. I thought he'd like it since it said *Ciao*. He shows up here wearing the shirt and didn't even recall I gave it to him. He didn't remember me at all."

"It was a long time ago—"

"Don't make excuses for him. He was a liar. He used people to get what he wanted. He told me I was special and talented when we were at Hillside Studios. We partied together, you know? I was thrilled knowing he would help me become famous like him. Then, after he left Hillside, I didn't hear from him again. But I waited. I knew he'd come back to me. I was so excited when Abby invited him to come to her studio. I thought Marco would finally see me as his peer when he arrived. Instead, he came in here and treated me like crap, and he treated Abby like crap as well. So insulting! All I wanted was for us to teach together—to be together—like we were supposed to be."

"Oh, Sam, that must've have been really hard—"

Sam cut me off. "And then, he put the moves on Katia. I couldn't stand it."

"But, she said no to his advances."

"Oh, but he would have changed her mind. Trust me—he had a way of getting what he wanted. Once he was gone, I thought everything would be fine, we could all move on. But then you went and got his brother. I could have taught the class. We didn't need another cocky Italian in here acting like God's gift to glassblowing."

"I'm sorry, I didn't realize you could've taught the class. How could any of us have known?"

"You should have known. Everyone should have known about me. I'm important, you understand," Sam said, holding the glass spike inches from my face. I could feel its radiant heat. He was going to burn me, or worse. Sam glanced at Tessa, unconscious on the floor. "Really, though, it's Tessa's fault, too. She's Italian, from some sort of big-name family. She was strutting around here. All those Venetians, acting like they're better than everyone else, just because they were born in Venice—that crappy tourist trap of an island." He thrust the spear at me, stopping short of touching my chest. I inhaled instinctively, trying to avoid the hot glass. There was a terrible, sick gleam in Sam's eyes.

"I know Tessa, and she's not like that. Tessa has never strutted a day in her life. She's the most down-to-earth person there is. I don't know the rest of them any better than you do, but they're decent people."

"Shut up! Just shut up! It's time for her to go. If she wakes up, it'll be the two of you against me. Even if she's small, she's smart." Sam dragged me to Tessa and pushed the punty into my hands. "And after you kill her, I think it'll be your turn to die. You had to go off and find Dez. I thought I'd taken care of him. I guess I'll have to try harder next time, because I won't let him tell the world what I did."

"I don't know what you're talking about, Sam. Let's just stop and talk about this. Calmly—"

"Come on, time for your final lesson, before the glass is too cool," Sam said, standing next to me, his hands holding the punty inches in front of mine as he guided the point of the hot blade toward Tessa's chest.

"Sam, please, we don't have to do this," I said, pulling back. His hands slipped an inch down the punty, but the searing tip remained dangerously close to Tessa. Tessa stirred and reached up to touch her head.

"Tessa! Don't move!" I needed to do something—anything— before she died the same awful way Marco had.

I closed my eyes, and with all my weight, pulled backward, falling away from Sam, the punty sliding through his hands until all he grasped was the searing-hot glass spike. Screaming, Sam released his grip and I landed on the floor a few feet away. I scrambled up, still holding the punty with the spike on its end.

Sam came toward me, screaming in pain. "Give me that thing!"

I looked around the studio. I needed to get rid of this glass spear before Sam could grab it from me. I ran to the water-filled crack-off bucket and plunged the hot glass in. It sizzled and exploded. The blade was gone—broken into a million pieces.

Sam reached for me with his blistering red hands. I turned and used the punty to hit the padlock on the roll-up door, trying to break it. Finally, the lock popped open, and I heaved the rolling door up.

"It's over, Sam," I said.

He collapsed onto the glassblower's bench. Whimpering, all his anger seemingly burned out of him, he examined his ruined hands, in shock.

I ran to Tessa. "Are you okay?"

"What happened?" Tessa asked, her eyes, unfocused.

"Stay still. I'll get help. Sam killed Marco, and he was about to kill you. But I put a stop to it."

Tessa pulled herself onto her elbows and spotted Sam anguishing over his hands. "We've got to get out of here."

A black patrol car sped toward us, skidding to a stop a few feet from the rolling door. It was Sheriff Harvey Poole, who leapt from his car, hoisting up his belt and drawing his gun. I never thought I'd be so glad to see that man again.

"You'll find the murderer of Marco de Luca inside," I said.

"You mean it's not you?"

"Sorry, no. I think you'll find Sam is willing to confess, but he may need a trip to the emergency room first."

Tessa came to my side and gripped my hand for support. Together we watched the sheriff attempt to cuff Sam, before giving up and guiding him to the patrol car. The sheriff turned on the cruiser's siren and lights and headed off into the darkness.

Tessa and I sat on the long bench in front of the studio.

"What now?" I asked. "I can't drive the Ladybug. Sam threw my keys out into the field and he tossed my phone in the furnace."

"Come on, I left my purse in the car. We'll get my phone and call Val," Tessa said.

"Before we do, I want to check something out."

We walked along the side of the building and passed through the utility yard to the double rolling doors. We slid the right door open and peered in. Inside were stacks of bags of glass, racks of tools, and glassblowing equipment. We rolled the left door open and found a pickup truck. I couldn't be certain, but I'd be willing to bet this was Sam's truck. And I wondered whether his front bumper had recently been replaced. It certainly looked newer than the rest of the beat up chassis.

I would make sure to share the news of this discovery with Zachary.

TWENTY-NINE

I STOPPED OVER AT TESSA'S a few days later to give her a box with gifts for her daughters. It was fantastic to see everything was back to normal.

"Come on up, and I'll show you the new bedroom." I followed my friend up the stairs.

The renovated attic was perfect. Where there once had been a plywood floor, there was now gleaming hardwood. The rough framing on the walls had been newly sheet-rocked and painted, and the open-beam ceiling added an airy touch to the room.

I noticed two twin beds placed side-by-side, one under each dormer.

"Why are there two beds up here? I thought only one girl was going to move."

"When it was time to move Izzy into her new room, the two girls got all weepy on me. It turned out that the concept of having separate rooms was more appealing than actually being apart. But there is a lot more space for them to share."

"I've got the perfect thing for these two beds." I opened the box I was holding and pulled out one of Great-Aunt Rita's exquisite handmade quilts, which Tessa and I had found in my attic. I shook it out and arranged it across one of the beds so we could see the whole thing.

"Oh, Jax, it's brilliant," Tessa said quietly, overwhelmed with the quilt's beauty. "Aren't you worried about giving them away?"

"I talked with Andy and Connie, and they both agreed that your girls should have the quilts. They'll be pleased to know the quilts are being used and enjoyed, not collecting dust in my attic."

"Instead, being used in mine."

"*Being used.* That's right. Precious handmade things deserve to be used and enjoyed." I pulled out the second quilt and spread it out on the other bed.

"As beautiful as the first!" Tessa said, admiring the perfect floral calico squares that comprised the quilt, reminding me of the floral patterns we'd seen in the millefiori beads this week. I had to admit that by sheer chance, the quilts I'd given the girls coordinated perfectly with the pale green paint Rudy had used on the walls in the room. "Thank you, Jax," Tessa said, giving me an enormous hug.

"So, what are you going to do with the extra bedroom the girls have left behind?" I asked.

"Same as you—I'm going to have my very own Bead Lair!"

"How did the girls like drama camp?"

"They loved it. Izzy had a lead role in 'Grease.' She was one of the Pink Ladies. It's all she's talked about since she got home. It turned out Ashley really liked working backstage on props, and she ended up as the show's stage manager."

"That's terrific. And the boys?"

"They loved their time at Camp Grammy and can't wait to go back, although I think Patsy may need a little help next time. She was exhausted after a nearly a week with Joey and Benny. Rosie and I are going to make her a special necklace as a thank-you gift."

"Any news from Old Firehouse Studio?"

"It sounds like Dez is recovering from his accident. Both of his legs were fractured in multiple places. It's going to be a while before he's walking again, but he's fortunate to be alive. According to Abby, he's working on staying sober."

"That's great news. What's going to happen to the studio now that Sam's gone?"

"Katia is going to help out in the hot shop, and from the sounds of it there may be some sort of a partnership forming—and I don't just mean professionally—between Katia and Dario."

"That's not surprising. She seemed smitten with him. Funny, she had such a different reaction with the two brothers."

"It's not surprising at all. I felt the same way about those two men. I never liked Marco, may he rest in peace, but Dario, I loved—"

"Loved?"

"Yes, Jax. I did love Dario, and I still do, but like a brother or a friend. With Marco and his parents gone, he could use the support of our family." Tessa had done the same for me when I moved to Seattle. Since my family was so far away, she had invited me into hers, and my life was richer because of it. "He brought something by for you. It's in the living room."

"What is it?" I asked, as we headed downstairs.

"I don't know. I guess you'll have to open it." Tessa handed me a tall box. Inside was a gorgeous vase covered in purple, green, and red murrine. I was certain Dario had made it himself. It took my breath away.

"Oh, Tessa. This is incredible."

"He brought me one, too." She pointed to another open box, the top of a vase sticking out of it.

"Why aren't you displaying it?"

"Because I want your brother to have it. He was so sweet to let us stay with him, and he helped us figure out what was going on with Vickie and Carl Nest. And most important—the man has no art in his entire apartment."

"That's very generous. I'm sure he'll love it."

• • •

That evening as I tidied up my studio, I came across the small whale sculpture I'd found in the trunk with the quilts. Holding it in my hands, I couldn't help but wonder about it. Why did my great-aunt save this treasure? I glanced up at the attic door. It was in need of renovation, especially with my nephew coming to visit in a few months. Tessa's attic update had inspired me, but funding such a large project would be a challenge. Mr. Chu was interested in buying the carving, and from what he said, it might fetch a hefty sum, perhaps even enough to pay for the remodel. But could I part with it? I wasn't sure. I felt it held the key to a mystery yet to be solved. I had some investigating to do before I was ready to let it go.

Val burst in my front door wearing a frilly light blue apron.

"Are you ready for some fried chicken?" Val asked, waving her kitchen tongs dramatically as she met me halfway down the hall.

"I do believe I am," I said, making a detour into my bedroom. "I'll be right there." I placed the tiny ivory whale on my bedside stand and whispered a silent thank-you to Aunt Rita for all she had given me.

"Don't be such a slowpoke," Val shouted from the living room.

I sped toward the door and followed Val over to her side of the duplex. Uncle Freddie was sitting at the dinner table having a glass of wine.

Val offered me a seat across from Freddie and went out to the kitchen to get me a drink.

"Here's some wine for you, Jax," Val said, handing me a glass and setting a plate heaped with biscuits on the table.

"Smells terrific!" Freddie said. "When do we get to eat?"

"When our other guests arrive," Val said.

"Other guests? Who—"

The doorbell rang and Val bustled to the door.

"For you, Ms. Roberts," said Zachary, handing her a small bouquet of yellow roses.

"Oh my! Please, call me Val," she said with a lady-like titter, taking the flowers and giving them a dainty sniff. "Come in, please. Here you are," Val said, patting the seat next to me.

Zachary sat down. He had another rose bouquet, this one red, still in his hands.

"I brought you this," Zachary said, handing me the flowers and looking at me a little longer than necessary.

"They're lovely. Thank you," I said, admiring the blossoms and placing the bouquet next to my plate.

"Zachary, this is Freddie, and Freddie, Zachary," I said introducing the men.

"Nice to meet you," Zachary said, unfazed by meeting one of the best rock-n-roll guitarists of all time. I subtly turned to Zachary and whispered, "Isn't it exciting to hang out with the great Freddie Roberts?"

"Seems like a nice guy," Zachary said. One of the many amazing things about Zachary was that he wasn't easily flustered, except when talking with women—or at least with me.

"How's everything going with Tessa?" Val asked.

"The top floor of her house is like new now that Rudy and the contractors are done. They slipped in under the deadline and just finished up a few hours before everyone got home."

"I'm glad they got done in time. Now Rudy can go to the convention with me next week. He's coming by in a little while to show me his costume. Do you want to see mine?"

Without waiting for an answer, Val trotted off to change. Minutes later, she reappeared in her flowing Princess Leia costume, complete with a wig that looked like she had a cinnamon bun over each ear. The dress was perfect for her curvy figure. She swished around the room so we could get a look at her from all sides.

"Fantastic! But what happened to the stormtrooper outfit?" I asked.

"You know, I couldn't make that work. I had all of this," Val gestured to her voluptuous figure, "and a hard, plastic shell just couldn't contain it."

That was the truth. Nothing could contain Val and her big personality. A few minutes later the doorbell rang, and in came Rudy in his authentic Luke Skywalker costume.

"Hey everyone. May the force be with you," Rudy said, owning his nerdy Star Wars attitude.

"Doesn't he look faboo?" Val asked.

"He does. But, I always thought he was more of a Han Solo

type," I said.

"I'm going to find a Han Solo to call my very own, so Rudy has to be someone else, like Luke. You see, Luke is Leia's brother, so that's sort of like Rudy. And then Han—"

"It's okay. You don't have to explain it to me." Val always had more to say about sci-fi than I had patience to hear.

I grabbed the bottle of chardonnay off the table and poured myself another glass.

"Would you like some?" I asked Freddie.

"Don't mind if I do." He took a sip "This is marvelous—buttery with a nutty afterglow."

Freddie was full of surprises—a rock legend and a wine connoisseur.

"Freddie, did you find that business opportunity you were looking for?" I asked.

"As a matter of fact, I did. It's a ways out of town from here. A funky little town called Carthage."

"Carthage!" Zachary and I said, astounded.

"I found a little café that's for sale. It looks like it would be an excellent business opportunity—you know, a way to cash in on my name. The couple wants to sell their restaurant and move closer to Tacoma."

"You're going to buy the Robin's Nest Café?" I asked.

"Yeah, you know it? I'm going to make it into a rock-n-roll themed restaurant. It's going to be awesome after I redecorate it with some of the memorabilia from my band's concert tours. I've already got some investors interested. I even found a little house to rent until I can build something custom."

This meant Carl and Vickie would finally be able to move closer to their daughter and afford the care she needed to completely rehabilitate. With the updated restaurant, along with more people visiting Carthage, I hoped that meant Old Firehouse Studio wouldn't struggle to find customers for their glass art and classes.

"Was it Sam who cut Dez's brake lines?" I asked Zachary.

"After being treated for his burns, Sam decided to confess to everything. He had gone to The Office with the hope of having an alibi after killing Marco. Apparently, Dez had been doing a little sleuthing of his own. He realized Sam was the culprit in the hit-and-run accident, and he confronted him at the bar."

"So, Sam tried to kill Dez to cover up the hit-and-run?" I asked.

"It appears to be the case. From the sound of it, Sam left the bar, sliced the brake lines of Dez's car in the parking lot and then figured that in combination with the large quantity of alcohol Dez consumed, it would lead to a fatal crash," Zachary said. "Thanks to you, Jax—you helped us find a connection between a damaged bumper at the car repair shop that matches the make and model of Sam Tilden's pickup, which you found in the storage unit behind Old Firehouse Studio. Tony Stein at the garage is going back through his records to check the timing of the repair to see if it coincides with the hit-and-run."

I was stunned. Zachary had actually thanked me for helping solve a crime.

"Wow. Did you just thank me?"

"Ahem, I uh—" Zachary sputtered. I leaned over and kissed him on the cheek.

"You're welcome. Do you think Sheriff Poole is grateful, too?"

"I wouldn't push your luck," he said with a smile.

There was a knock at the front door. Val opened it and ushered in Ryan Shaw. I waved and smiled, although I felt awkward seeing him.

"Hello, Officer Shaw." Zachary rose and shook Ryan's hand. Zachary's grip might have been a little firmer than was absolutely necessary, judging by the twinge of pain that crossed Ryan's face.

"Uh, well, actually, it's no longer Officer Shaw," Ryan said. "I've officially left the Seattle Police Department."

My jaw dropped.

"I had a few infractions and, well, as a new officer, the higher-ups didn't think much of my actions going above and beyond the call of duty." He'd overstepped the limits of his position, so I wasn't surprised to hear Ryan's commanding officers were unhappy with some of his questionable actions, including handing me a *Get Out of Jail Free* card.

We all mumbled our condolences.

"But—I've already got something new lined up, thanks to Val and her Uncle Freddie."

"What?" I asked.

"Personal security for Freddie. Thanks for introducing me to him, Val. Of course, Jax, you're the one who sent me over here in the first place, so I guess I owe you my gratitude as well."

"You're going to be Freddie's bodyguard?"

Freddie nodded. "That's right. And all-around personal assistant."

Incredible. Absolutely incredible. I could say one thing about Ryan, he certainly knew how to land on his feet.

"I came by to pick up your suitcases and take them out to your new place," Ryan said to Freddie. The two men headed to Val's spare room, grabbed the bags, and Ryan was on his way out the door. I was relieved he wasn't staying. It was a little too awkward having both Ryan and Zachary in the same room with each other, the tension between them nearly palpable.

I studied Rudy in his Luke Skywalker costume, looking every bit as authentic as Val did, and I was certain they'd fit right in at the Burien UFO Festival. He had settled in at the table and struck up a conversation with Freddie while Val, having loaded the table with dishes of mashed potatoes, green beans with almonds, and a platter of delicious fried chicken, whipped off her apron and plopped into the chair next to Rudy.

"To friends," Val said, raising her wine glass.

"And family," Uncle Freddie added.

"To friends and family," Zachary and I chimed in.

We dug in to Val's feast and it was every bit as delicious as we hoped it would be. Her cooking skills had definitely improved.

"And now the grand finale," Val said, heading to the kitchen for dessert. She returned with an enormous carrot cake.

"I don't know about you, but I don't think I can eat another bite. So, what do you say I play you guys a few songs until we're ready for dessert?" Freddie asked, grabbing his guitar case from beside the sofa.

"Absolutely," I said. "I think we should go out to my back patio."

The rain had finally stopped and the sky was clear. We dragged some chairs outside. Freddie sat on the studio steps and started strumming his guitar. We listened to him play all of our favorite rock songs, singing along at times. After a while, Mr. Chu came out, stood on his back porch with a longhaired calico in his arms, and listened, too. Val retrieved the cake from her kitchen, and gave us each a slice. She took one across the alley and gave it to Mr. Chu, who smiled appreciatively and may have decided—just a little—that people weren't so bad, after all.

"And now, I'm going to sing one for my favorite four-footed friends," Freddie said, playing the first few chords of Elvis Presley's "Hound Dog."

"Ah-roo!" Stanley howled in appreciation. We all joined in singing and howling along with Freddie and the dog.

It was a marvelous way to end a week that had not been what I'd expected. I'd learned some things about myself—for one, I'd never be a glassblower, but I was content to be a glass beadmaker for as long as I could. Zachary reached over and grasped my hand as we swayed to the music on this starlit night and pulled me toward him. It was a wonderful night for kissing, and maybe a little bit more.

ACKNOWLEDGMENTS

I want to give an enormous thank-you to all the wonderful and patient people who have helped me make this book a reality. Thanks to my beta reading team, whose early feedback on my manuscript is greatly appreciated. A huge thanks goes out to Ellen Margulies, my supportive editor, who finds all the little—and not so little—problems that I simply can't see when I'm hip-deep in words. Thanks to David Patchen, a talented glass artist who uses murrine in all of his gorgeous work, for helping with the glassblowing details in this book. Thanks, as well, to beadologist Frederick Chavez for his advice on antique Venetian beads, including the information he gathered from the smart folks at beadcollector.net. I want to give a shout out to Jim and Karen O'Malley who have kept me on the up-and-up when it comes to P.D. and 911 procedures for all of my books.

And last, but certainly not least, my love and thanks to Jeff Peacock, the best husband I've ever had. (Also, the only husband I've ever had.) He has always believed in me, and for that, I am forever grateful.

ABOUT THE AUTHOR

Janice Peacock decided to write her first mystery novel after working in a glass studio full of colorful artists who didn't always get along. They reminded her of the quirky and often humorous characters in the murder mystery books she loves to read. Inspired by that experience, she combined her two passions and wrote *High Strung*, the first book in the Glass Bead Mystery Series featuring glass beadmaker Jax O'Connell. Janice has continued the series with *A Bead in the Hand*, and *Be Still My Beading Heart, A Glass Bead Mini-Mystery*.

When Janice isn't writing about glass artists-turned-amateur-detectives, she creates glass beads using a torch, designs one-of-a-kind jewelry, and makes sculptures using hot glass. Her work has been exhibited internationally and is in the permanent collections of the Corning Museum of Glass, the Glass Museum of Tacoma, WA, and in private collections worldwide.

Janice lives in the San Francisco Bay Area with her husband, two cats, and an undisclosed number chickens. She has a studio full of beads...lots and lots of beads.

CONNECT WITH JANICE PEACOCK

www.JanicePeacock.com
jp@janicepeacock.com

Sign up for Janice's newsletter at
www.janicepeacock.com/newsletter

www.facebook.com/janpeac
Twitter, Instagram, Pinterest:
@JanPeac

Did you enjoy this book?
Please write a review on the website where you purchased it

MORE BOOKS IN THE GLASS BEAD MYSTERY SERIES

HIGH STRUNG
Glass Bead Mystery Series
Book One

After inheriting a house in Seattle, Jax O'Connell is living the life of her dreams as a glass beadmaker and jewelry designer. When she gets an offer to display her work during a bead shop's opening festivities, it's an opportunity Jax can't resist—even though the store's owner is the surliest person Jax has ever met.

The weekend's events become a tangled mess when a young bead-maker is found dead nearby and several oddball bead enthusiasts are suspects. Jax must string together the clues to clear her friend Tessa's name—and do it before the killer strikes again.

Also available in audio book and ebook formats.

A BEAD IN THE HAND
Glass Bead Mystery Series
Book Two

A bead bazaar turns bizarre when jewelry designer and glass bead-maker Jax O'Connell discovers a dead body beneath her sales table. Suspected of murder, Jax and her friend Tessa scramble to find the killer among the fanatic shoppers and eccentric vendors. They have their hands full dealing with a scumbag show promoter, hipsters in love, and a security guard who wants to do more than protect Jax from harm. Adding to the chaos, Jax's quirky neighbor Val arrives unexpectedly with trouble in tow. Can Jax untangle the clues before she's arrested for murder?

Also available in audio book and ebook formats.

TO BEAD OR NOT TO BEAD
Glass Bead Mystery Series
Book Four

Glass beadmaker Jax O'Connell and her friend Tessa have no idea
When a wealthy theater owner is killed by a falling art glass chande-
lier, glass beadmaker Jax O'Connell's boyfriend, Detective Zachary
Grant, quickly determines it was no accident. Jax and her friend
Tessa try to carry on with a charity fashion gala at the theater, but
with only a few days before the big event, they have to scramble
to keep things from falling apart. The emcee quits, and to make
matters worse, Tessa's daughters are suspects in the murder. As the
chaos unfolds, Jax discovers new suspects at every turn, including
an edgy glass blower, an agoraphobic socialite, and a hunky former-
cop-turned-actor. Can Jax piece together the clues to find the killer
and uncover the dark secrets behind the victim's family or will it be
curtains for her?

Also available in audio book and ebook formats.

BE STILL MY BEADING HEART
A Glass Bead Mini-Mystery

It's Valentine's Day and Jax O'Connell's red VW bug is missing. Did she forget where she parked The Ladybug as she rushed to deliver her handmade glass beads, or has the beloved car been stolen? Searching the streets of Seattle, Jax and her best friend, Tessa, face some unsavory characters. Jax regrets not having a date on the most romantic day of the year after spotting Ryan, Seattle's newest—and hottest—cop and running into Zachary, the stern yet sexy detective. She must take matters into her own hands to find The Ladybug and salvage her love life, and do it before the day is over. This stand-alone short story features the quirky characters of the Glass Bead Mystery Series and is available as an ebook.

9 780990 570592